Fire Island

A Novel

John J. Stevens

West Islip Public Library
3 Higbie Lane
West Islip, New York 11795

FireIslandNovel.com

Copyright

Fire Island
By John J. Stevens

Copyright 2010, John J. Stevens. All rights reserved. No part of this book may be reproduced or retransmitted in any form or by any means without the written permission of the publisher.

Published by:

Bullfrog Communications, Inc.
25 Hofstra Drive
Greenlawn, NY 11740
eBullfrog.com

Printed by:

Lightning Source
An Ingram Content Group Company
1246 Heil Quaker Blvd.
La Vergne, TN USA 37086

At the website **FireIslandNovel.com**, you can purchase additional print copies or eBook versions of *Fire Island*. There you can also find additional text and media about the book, the time period, and the surfmen.

International Standard Book Number (ISBN) - 978-0-615-40156-0

Library of Congress Control Number: 2010913398

FireIslandNovel.com

Dedication

"Thank you God for instilling in me the desire to write this book; may it be also that You instill the desire in others to read it."

Contents

Introduction i-1
Chapter One - The Capitalist 1
Chapter Two - The Night Awakes 5
Chapter Three - The Mooncussers 11
Chapter Four - Young America 15
Chapter Five - The Wreckmasters 21
Chapter Six - Lost at Sea 23
Chapter Seven - Fire In the Sky 27
Chapter Eight - Fire and Ice 29
Chapter Nine - Beach Pirates 33
Chapter Ten - Up The Masts 35
Chapter Eleven - On the Beach 39
Chapter Twelve - Scuttle 43
Chapter Thirteen - The White Shroud 45
Chapter Fourteen - The Vigil 49
Chapter Fifteen - The Longest Night 51
Chapter Sixteen - The Aftermath 55
Chapter Seventeen - The Spoils 58
Chapter Eighteen - At Cassandra's House 59
Chapter Nineteen - At Grinnell's House 63
Chapter Twenty - Wild, Strong and Beautiful 69
Chapter Twenty-One - The Ol' Stand 73
Chapter Twenty-Two - Blood Money 77
Chapter Twenty-Three - Abraham Century 83
Chapter Twenty-Four - The Red Book 87
Chapter Twenty-Five - The Party 91
Chapter Twenty-Six - By the Light of Her Eyes 95
Chapter Twenty-Seven - The Service 99
Chapter Twenty-Eight - There The Dragons Be 103

Chapter Twenty-Nine - When Half-Gods Go	107
Chapter Thirty - On the Street of Ships	115
Chapter Thirty-One - A Visit from Joshua James	121
Chapter Thirty-Two - Fire in the Mind	127
Chapter Thirty-Three - The Mute Sea	131
Chapter Thirty-Four - Commission of the Station House	135
Chapter Thirty-Five - Fire in the Heart	143
Chapter Thirty-Six - The Association Meeting	147
Chapter Thirty-Seven - Trask Leaves Cassandra's Care	151
Chapter Thirty-Eight - Sabotage	157
Chapter Thirty-Nine - Trask Joins the Service	161
Chapter Forty - Her Walk With Emerson	165
Chapter Forty-One - The Introduction of the Lyle Gun	169
Chapter Forty-Two - Three-Finger Riley	173
Chapter Forty-Three - On the Beach	181
Chapter Forty-Four - Wailing in the Wind	189
Chapter Forty-Five - Ship Ashore!	193
Chapter Forty-Six - Men in the Rigging	197
Chapter Forty-Seven - Eck	202
Chapter Forty-Eight - Darkness	203
Chapter Forty-Nine - The Launch of the Life Boat	207
Chapter Fifty - Save!	215
Chapter Fifty-One - I Want To Go Home	219
Epilogue - The Funeral of Abraham Century	221
About the Author	227
About the Illustrations	228
Bibliography	229

Preface

One night, as part of a group of visitors on Fire Island, I was treated to a tale-well-told by a National Park Service Ranger, who, around a bonfire on the beach, told us of the heroic Surfmen who long ago patrolled those shores looking to save shipwreck survivors. In my mind's eye, I still see her face: lit by the glow of the fire, topped with her Ranger's stout-brimmed cap, sparks flying off, then disappearing, into the blackness around her.

That evening catapulted me into the writing of this novel, about an epic time in American history, and some of the people who made it so.

This is a book of faction, (as opposed to *fiction*) in that, some of the people and events described herein represent real people and events of the time, and some of the people and events are representational of the time.

The character Joshua James, for example, is based on a real surfman of that name from the period. James is considered to be the greatest life-saver of all time, and is credited for saving more than 1,000 people off the coast of Hull, Massachusetts. The main character William Trask, on the other hand, is fictional, and is based on composite attributes of sea captains of the day.

There is mention herein of the wreck of the *Louis V. Place*, which was in fact an infamous shipwreck off Fire Island. But the actual wreck occurred in 1895. It's occurrence in this story, however, is placed much earlier in time.

Hence, *faction*.

Foreword

"You have to go out; but you don't have to come back."

The motto of the United States Lifesaving Service

"God always forgives;

Man sometimes forgives;

Nature never forgives."

Acknowledgments

To the following people, please accept my heartfelt gratitude for reading initial versions of this story, and giving me your helpful insight into how I might make it better:

Marie Stevens

Paul Stevens

Karen Bobetsky

Bob Hyne

Bill Perks

Steve Scrobe

Donald Hehir

Professor Margaret Brown

Thank you, also, Gina Bivona and Michael Malusa for laying out the pages.

Fire Island

FIRE ISLAND

JOHN J. STEVENS

Introduction

In 1857, America is first striding onto the stage of elite nations, like a cocky 17-year-old boy, bristling with energy, without much history, shoulders square to the future, never having lost in his life.

The Revolutionary War had ended some 80 years earlier, and the liberty unleashed by that event is still surging through the American system, like testosterone in that 17-year-old boy.

In that year, about 25 million people live in the U.S., about as many as live in New York State today. This number represents an astounding 35% increase in population since the census of 1840 less than two decades earlier. It is the fastest rate of growth the country has ever experienced, before or since.

Eighty-five percent of these citizens live in rural areas.

Steam-driven trains are transforming life - speeding up commerce, cargo and information. Railroad tracks are opening up access to new parts of the country at a breathtaking rate. In May of 1851, the Erie Railroad opens. In 1853, the railroad goes from New York to Chicago; 1854, the railroad reaches the Mississippi River. In 1856, the first rail bridge across the Mississippi River (from Rock Island to Davenport) is built; the West is now open to rail traffic.

The nation is now fully committed to the concept of Manifest Destiny, the growing sense that the U.S. is destined to occupy the continent from sea to shining sea. It was 27 years earlier, in 1830, when President Jackson signed the Great Removal act, forcibly resettling all Indians west of the Mississippi.

At the time, Jackson addressed the nation thusly: "What good man would prefer a country covered with forests, and ranged by a few thousand savages to our extensive Republic, studded with cities, towns, and prosperous farms, embellished with all the improvements which art can devise or industry execute?"

Women cannot vote in 1857. Indeed, some three-quarters of men are also ineligible to participate in this most basic of democratic acts.

The U.S. Flag features 31 stars.

Over three million people live as slaves in the southern states. Even in New York State, as late as 1820, slaves constitute one-sixth of the population of the agricultural communities of Kings County (Brooklyn).

In 1852, Frederick Douglass suggests that black Americans have no reason to celebrate the Fourth of July; as long as blacks are enslaved, he reasons, there is no Independence Day.

There is no income tax.

The legal age of consent in New York is ten years of age.

It was only 13 years earlier, May 24, 1844, that the first telegraph message is sent from Washington, DC, to Baltimore, Maryland.

If you want to communicate with someone far off, you write a letter. It might arrive in a week or so. It would be two more years until the first cross-country mail would be delivered.

It has only been 15 years since the Child Labor Law in Massachusetts (passed in 1842) limited the workday to 10 hours for children under 12.

1842 is also the year that marks the first use of ether to kill pain during an operation (Dr. Crawford Long in Georgia). Dentistry is a luxury, affordable only by the few. If you need a tooth pulled, you go to the barber, or the blacksmith who uses a "pullekin" to remove the offending tooth. No anesthesia is administered; no infection control, no attempt to control the bleeding.

Death is an obvious part of life in 1857. At the beginning of the

19th century life expectancy is about 37 years; by the 1860s this has improved to 40.3 years.

Between 1850 and 1860, more than half of those under the age of five die each year - seven of every 10 under the age of two. Cholera races through the tenements in New York City in 1852. Typhus, an immigrant disease passed along easily because of overcrowding, grows endemic, then epidemic in 1852. Deaths from consumption (tuberculosis) soar in the black and immigrant communities.

Overseas, death is also on a vigorous march. From 1845 to 1849, when the potato crop fails, more than a million Irish die of starvation. Many of them take their chances with typhus, cholera and consumption in New York.

There are pigs and hogs everywhere on the streets of New York. In 1849, the police flush 5,000 - 6,000 pigs out of cellars and garrets, and drive an estimated 20,000 swine north to the upper wards that summer. Most dogs are killed in the street by small boys with clubs.

In New York City, up until the middle of the 19th century, most sewage is disposed in backyard outhouses, dumped into the gutter, or poured into ponds and streams that still exist in Manhattan. But, in 1849, prompted by a series of cholera outbreaks, the first 70 miles of the New York City sewer system is built. These are combined sewers into which run human waste *and* rainwater. The rainwater flushes the human waste through the pipes to the outflow into the surrounding rivers and harbors.

The mean educational level at the time is the eighth grade.

In 1846, in New Jersey, at the Elysian Fields, the first game of baseball using recognizable rules is played.

Sail power in 1857 is roughly equivalent to what nuclear power is today in that, having it automatically enrolls a country in the elite of nations.

At this time, the world is just taking notice of America's sailing prowess. The shipyards of Manhattan crank out a steady stream of bigger, faster and prettier boats than anything theretofore seen.

In 1845, the *Rainbow*, a pioneer New York Clipper built at the shipyard of Smith & Dimon, New York, reaches Hong Kong in 89 days, having sailed against a monsoon. She romps home in 88 days, bringing the news of her own arrival.

In 1851, the *America*, a radically designed black schooner from the New York Yacht Club, captained by Commodore John Cox Stevens, defeats *Aurora* and 13 other British vessels in the Race of Nations around the Isle of Wight.

Stevens sails home with the One Hundred Guinea Cup, which becomes known as America's Cup. Britannia no longer rules the waves.

The clipper, *Flying Cloud*, built in New York in 1854, performs the incredible feat of sailing to San Francisco around Cape Horn in 89 days, eight hours. This makes national news, smashing all previous records.

A young man named Cornelius Vanderbilt begins his career as a steamboat captain in the archipelago that is New York. He brawls and bullies his way into the key profitable routes around the city, and later parlays his winnings into a virtual monopoly of rail lines across the country. He starts at age 16 with a $100 loan from his mother; in 1879, he leaves an estate of $103 million, the most ever bequeathed in history at the time. "I have been insane on the subject of moneymaking all my life," Vanderbilt is quoted as saying in the year before he dies. And there are others like him: Andrew Carnegie, J.P. Morgan...all New Yorkers.

Again, no income taxes; also, no inheritance taxes, no anti-trust statutes.

The better part of the goods coming and going throughout the entire country passes through New York Harbor. If you walked up the East River from the Battery northward, you would likely see hundreds of ships at dock on the Manhattan and Brooklyn side of the East River, and on the Hudson River side of Manhattan. (Then, also known as the North River.)

Roughly 60,000 crewmen (oystermen, steamboat deckhands, sailors from whalers and naval vessels, canal boatmen) pass through town each year by the late 1850s.

Yet there are grave hazards to shipping and commerce in these days. The 10-mile stretch of ocean off Fire Island, the tidal island off Long Island, just east of New York City, becomes known as Wreck Valley, for the frequency of shipwrecks that occur there. In the 30-month period between from November 1854 to June 1857, 64 ships are either wrecked or in distress along this stretch. Walking along the beach at this time, one would seldom be out of sight of a wreck. From 1850 - 1870, 512 people perish in shipwrecks off the shores of Long Island and New Jersey, including author and champion of Women's Rights, Margaret Fuller. Communications are primitive; lighthouses are few. The average length of service for a seaman is seven years.

In 1849, there are fewer than 20 millionaires in the U.S. (Sixty years later, there would be over 20 in the U.S. Senate.) The disparity between the high and low class is obvious and growing.

What comes to be known as the Astor Place Riot takes place on the night of May 10, 1849, in which a mob of 20,000 working class men riots outside of a performance before upper class patrons at the Astor Place Opera House in New York City, resulting in at least 22 deaths and 150 injuries. The riot sharply defines the line between the haves and the have-nots in New York.

This is part of the push-back to the crass commercial activity of New York and the country. Flourishing are Utopian communities, religious movements, and the Transcendentalism epitomized by Ralph Waldo Emerson, Henry David Thoreau and Walt Whitman. In 1847, Brook Farm, a transcendental utopian community, is begun in Massachusetts, with Emerson, Nathaniel Hawthorne, Fuller, and many others active in it at some point. The author of *Little Women*, Louisa May Alcott, lives here as child.

"Great Awakening" religious revivals are sweeping the cities. Lydia Child writes that "everywhere, the old lines of thought seem to be undergoing a process of decomposition, and entering into new combinations."

Reform movements in health, women's rights, and temperance continue to build.

In late July of 1846, Thoreau spends a night in jail for refusing to pay his "poll tax." He refuses because he objects to his tax money being used to help support the enforcement of slavery laws, and finance the war with Mexico over Texas. Indeed, when an anonymous benefactor immediately pays the tax on his behalf, he is furious, and insists that he remain in jail.

The experience of being jailed prompts Thoreau to write what becomes one of the most influential political essays ever written, "On the Duty of Civil Disobedience."

"...I do not hesitate to say, that those who call themselves abolitionists should at once effectively withdraw their support, both in person and property, from the government of Massachusetts, and not wait till they constitute a majority of one, before they suffer the right to prevail through them...Moreover, any man more right than his neighbors, constitutes a majority of one already."

This essay becomes the handbook of non-violent protest, referenced over a century later by the likes of Mahatma Gandhi, Martin Luther King, Jr. and Supreme Court Justice William O. Douglas.

Real political reforms are launched in New York. Unions are developing to counterweight the growing wealth and influence of corporations. The abolition movement seeks to eliminate slavery.

This altruistic impulse is as much a part of the American character as that of the commercial. It manifests itself in the volunteer humanitarian societies that form to rescue and comfort survivors of shipwrecks, and the families of those who didn't survive the wrecks.

Out of those societies grows the United States Lifesaving Service, an early federal effort to formalize these volunteers into a type of civil service, much like today's fire-fighting companies. The men hired are employed from October to May each year, the storm season. They perform drills, walk a "beach watch" at night, and, when called upon, execute dramatic rescues of shipwreck survivors, often in the midst of the most ferocious storms.

In 1915, the United States Lifesaving Service merges with the Revenue Cutter Service to become the United States Coast Guard.

This is a story about the origins of the United States Lifesaving

Service, and some of the people of the time who helped to make America what it was then, and what it is today.

FIRE ISLAND

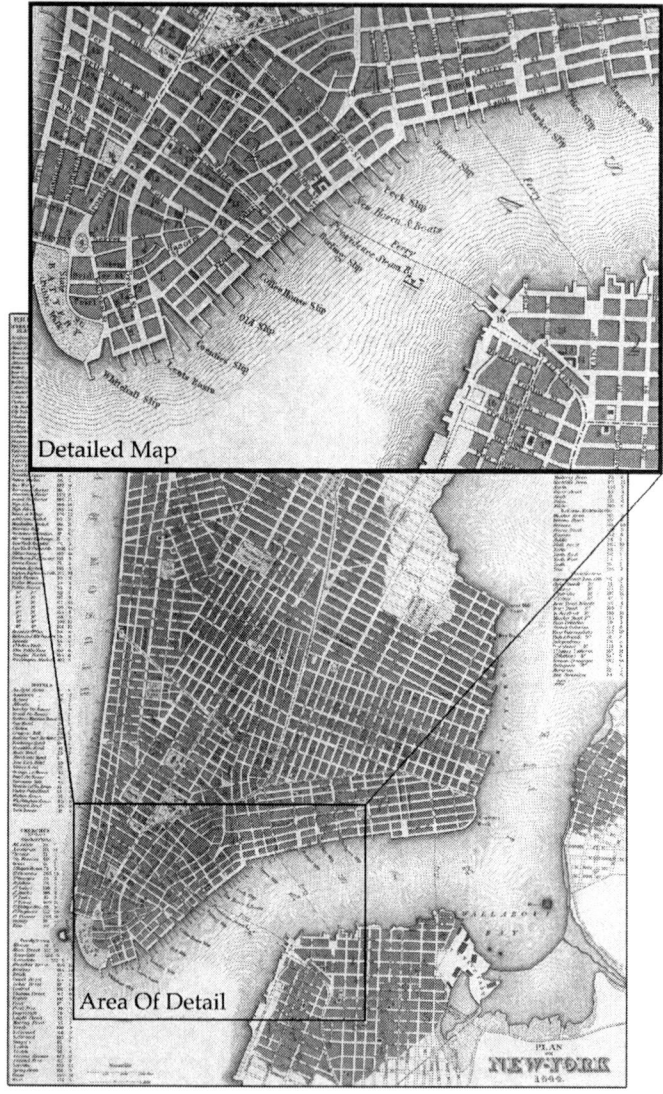

Map Of Lower Manhattan - 1844
Courtesy of Cartography Associates. David Rumsey Map Collection
www.davidrumsey.com

JOHN J. STEVENS

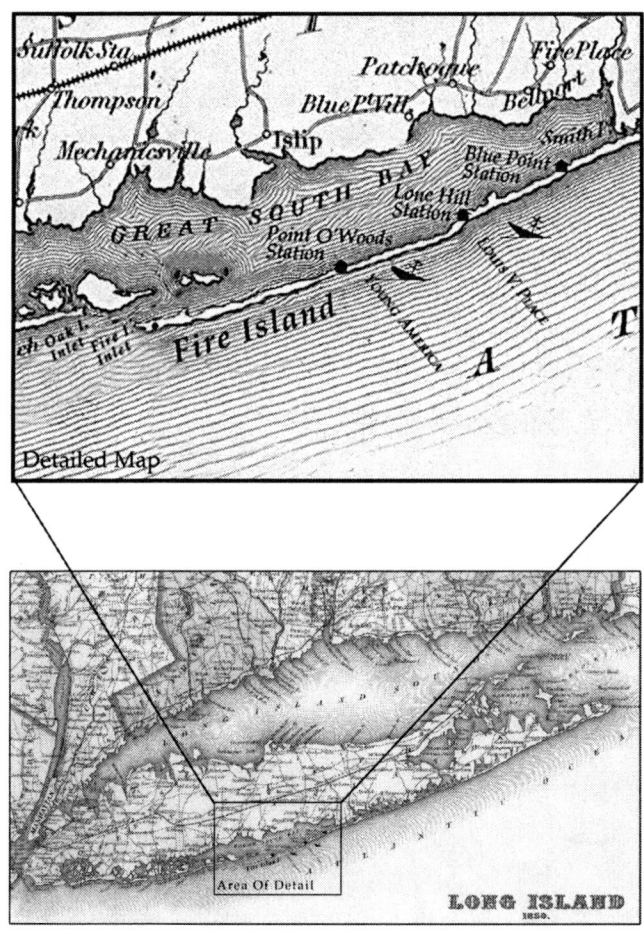

Map Of Long Island- 1850
Courtesy of Cartography Associates. David Rumsey Map Collection
www.davidrumsey.com

FIRE ISLAND

Esmerelda

Chapter One

The Capitalist

The air hung heavy on Manhattan like a wreath of poison. Moses Howland Grinnell brings the spyglass to his eye...
There - at the Battery - the tallest maple, his most reliable indicator as to the force and direction of the wind. Not a quiver in the leaves...

Overnight, something had changed. The forecast had been correct: a Nor'east'r is brewing, not uncommon in November, the height of the winter storm season, but troubling nevertheless. The wind would be coming from the Northeast by noon.

Grinnel turned to look east toward Brooklyn...The *Esmeralda*! Of course! Elias Miniturn had mentioned its imminent arrival at their last meeting. Grinnell paused awhile to watch the crew of the mighty craft at work as they set to it on the sails. It is a splendid vessel, and Miniturn ran a tight and tidy operation. But it isn't sailing very well right now. Indeed, if not for the oarsmen towing the *Esmeralda* in, she would be dead in the water within shouting distance of the shore with nothing but the tide to move her.

For the *Esmeralda*, her timing couldn't be better. She would be snug at harbor, just 12 hours or so before it really started to blow. But, for the *Young America*, Grinnell's vessel now exactly four days overdue from the China trade, her timing was far worse.

Grinnell leaves the scene of the *Esmeralda*'s docking, and steps up the pace of his morning constitution. In five minutes, he will reach the ramparts of the Battery on the southern tip of Manhattan Island.

At this hour, 5:45 a.m., Grinnell is a familiar sight in lower New York. His carriage is erect; his step, firm; his outfit, always the same, a dramatic black cape tied around his neck reaching to his leather boots. His shirt is closed at the neck, with a white stock, embroidered with his initials, MHG. His close-fitting pantaloons are outfitted with shiny gold regalia. A high stovepipe hat perched upon his head completes the outfit of this imposing man.

His early morning walk served a double function: exercise and fresh air for him, and an advanced look at the quantity and quality of goods the merchants and shopkeepers had "in store" for the day.

Grinnell passed a row of shops with which he did a considerable portion of his business. The firm of LeRoy, McEvers and Braynard had in cotton - good quality. Miniturn and Chaplain had in tea - a stack of aromatic chests, newly discharged, filled the shop floor. The principal, John Chaplain, of late, had been pushing the concept of fire insurance, a novel idea, yet one whose time had come, considering the many and devastating fires that have visited the First Ward. A fresh shipment is in at the huge counting house of Post and Russell on 70 South Street - cotton and rice, New Orleans sugar, Kentucky tobacco, molasses, raisins and spices. Serving the trade, some of the houses were full of ship chandlery - great cables, clocks, anchors and wheels, sail lofts occupied many of the upper stories of these three-storied buildings.

But it was the spectacle of the ships at dock that never failed to impress Grinnell. He paused for a moment, and looked north up the East River. There, side by side, he saw some 600 ships at dock on the Manhattan side of the river. Across the river on the Brooklyn side, there were at least another 70. The sight continued for as far as the eye could see. The morning sky by the water's edge was a forest of tall masts, spars, lines and flags.

For Grinnell, there was an air of the sacred to the scene - this astonishing number of vessels, representing the greater portion of trade for the entire nation, juxtaposed with the quiet of the early morning hour. Square-riggers from every port in the world poked their long bowsprits across South Street, almost ramming them into the third-story windows of the shops across the way. Grinnell walked stoutly under the arcade formed by the massive jib-booms of these lordly ships.

Grinnell was familiar with each one of the vessels. His firm, the Grinnell & Fish Trading Company, owned five - two at dock here, the packets *Perseverance* and the *Southerner*; the *Orient*, by this day, surely at dock in Shanghai, in trade with Houqua, the Hong merchant; the *Celestial*, at dock in Venezuela; and the *Young America*, overdue on its trip back from the China trade. It was the *Young America* that was on Grinnell's mind.

The Smell of a New Nation

Even at this hour, all was not quiet on this street of ships. On the *Pegoria*, the men were rousing from their quarters on-board. A doleful Indiaman peered over the railing of the massive vessel. He solemnly lifted a great cask, and walked it forward.

Dockside, two crusty teamsters, still fogged with sleep, drove their listless horses, pulling their dray newly laden with fragrant bales of cotton. Stevedores were unloading great casks of port sherry.

Vessels in every stage of completion slumbered in ways, like mighty Gullivers being built by Lilliputians. Grinnell could smell the freshly-cut stacks of white oak, live oak, locust and cedar in the yards. The powerful scent of pitch, tar and burning coke in the blacksmith's forges, now just fired up, stirred Grinnell's heart...

This was the smell of a new nation - a free, proud, and hard-working people. It was the smell of burgeoning confidence, of optimism, of enterprise. It seemed as if the very air shimmered with promise.

Grinnell observed the tide - higher than usual for the onset of an ebb tide, considerably higher.

Through the spyglass, he scanned the horizon, out through the Narrows. The harbor is calm and quiet, making about as much noise as the blood flowing through his veins. First light is brightening the sky from the east a lighter shade of blue. He turned the spyglass toward the East, Staten Island, to check the semaphore, or "telegraph" poles there. This signal system, funded by the Merchant's Association, would tell him, through a code of colored signal balls, all the shipping news, the comings and going of his fellow merchant's vessels.

Had the red and white colors for the *Young America* been hoisted, it would mean the lookout for the Narrows had spied his ship. From there it would be quick work to bring the vessel in. With a hand in the air and a whistle, the boatmen from the Whitehall Slip would be at their oars, ready to row out, and meet the incoming vessel. The sight of it, one's ship literally "coming in," was a joy and a relief that Moses Howland Grinnell's eyes yearned to see.

The green and white of Miniturn's *Esmeralda* are posted, but the red and white for the *Young America* are not on display. Grinnell lowered his spyglass. His eyes squinted, unaided, into the Narrows again. No sign of it - no relief - for Moses Howland Grinnell this day, November 23rd, 1857...

Chapter Two

The Night Awakes

During the day, the sea shows you its surface, and hardly that, for it reflects the world of day back to your eyes. The sea at night is a black-backed mirror of a speckled black dome - the night sky - and it disguises this with bewildering, shifting patterns of shadow and moonlight.
So, during the day, the sea reveals little, but at night, it reveals only a black beyond the black of shadows, and a suggestion of the endless dark and undulating plain, the surface of the water that stretches out into the nothingness beyond one's sight.

"What's your heading Hammerschmidt?"
"15 degrees northeast."
"Wind speed?"
"Must be 20 knots steady, now, with gusts up to 35 or so."
"Barometer?"
Hammerschmidt glances at the gauge. He leans over, wipes the moisture off the glass face, and takes a closer look.
"Twenty-eight degrees," he says, "and dropping like a stone."
Captain William I. H. Trask holds the spyglass to his eye, and aims it at an ugly sight. These aren't just rain clouds he's tracking. It is already raining, after all; had been, in fact, for almost two hours. No, this was the very wrath of God in the sky, black and angry, hell-bent on vengeance. It's a Nor'east'r in full fury, bearing down on his vessel like a locomotive.

With grim fascination, he stares at the billowing folds of this terrible beauty. Trask lowers his spyglass, wipes off the lens with this coat sleeve, and raises it again toward the unrestrained monster. Watching it approach over an open expanse of ocean is like watching the coming of the apocalypse...

The *Young America* is approaching the eastern coast of the United States, about 45 miles east of her destination, New York Harbor. She is about three miles south of Fire Island.

Fire Island is a long narrow coastal barrier island running parallel to Long Island, just to the east of New York Harbor. It is little more than a sand bar, really, dished up by the relentless ocean. Fire Island is also notoriously bad for harbors. It is a 70 mile stretch of virtually unbroken beachhead.

Trask knows there will be no hiding from this storm, but he does have some options. He can anchor, and drop the sails, hope to hunker through the worst of it, but, at this point, it is too early to choose this course of action, and the *Young America* would likely capsize. He could "feather" the vessel directly into the wind, hoping to ride out the storm, but, again, not yet. Or he could drop the sails completely, and leave the wooden hulk at the mercy of the elements. Only as a final option, he decides. With surf like this, without sails, there'd be no control over the ship.

No, at this point, the choice of action is clear. Run a broad reach, close-sailed in the wind shadow of Fire Island, and try to hold it together till they reach the Port of New York.

This won't be easy. The sea is already choppy, rolling, gray-green. Indeed, the chop of the surf had tipped the weather's hand 24 hours ago when the captain first knew it was going to blow. He'd used the power of the wind to his advantage, then. Running before the storm, every sail full to bursting, the bow of the *Young America* plunged deeply into the surf on every roll, every hand working, straight through, without break.

But now the rain was icing the entire vessel - the lines, the deck, the blocks, the steering wheel. Even Trask's beard had gone to white.

It had been a 7,000 mile sail from Shanghai. The crew had been out to sea and back for eight months now. The *Young America* was *so* close to safe harbor...

Of this, he reminded the crew.

"Not long to go now," he shouted at one point to no one and everyone. "No time to rest. We'll all rest when we get to port."

Trask knew these waters well. He had, quite literally, been born upon them. His parents, wayfarers from Sweden, had rescued an old scow from a boneyard in Stockholm, restored it, and sailed to America.

The passage, by way of the West Indies, had been well-blessed by sunshine, stout winds, and an uncommon bond among two people. Indeed, his father often said that, though they had been married for four years, it was on this trip that he had truly fallen in love with his wife.

Somewhere near the 38th parallel, in the middle of the Atlantic Ocean, during an uncommon 30-day stretch of fair weather, William was born. His father liked to say that the first thing his son laid eyes on was a sail full of wind.

Indeed, it seems, William I. H. Trask had been favored by the gods even before he was born. His physical gifts were uncommon - a long straight nose, jubilant eyes, blond hair upon which light danced and sparkled like the reflections of the sun on the water. His chest was broad, and the muscles in his stomach rippled like the ribs of a vessel under construction. Shaking his hand was like grabbing a coarse pumice rock. They were rough and callused from the years he spent building boats in the shipyard of Adam and Noah Brown.

There, Trask had established incredible records of performance and endurance. At 12, he was the youngest apprentice ever taken on. At 14, he was the youngest to attain journeyman status. His seniors were forced to acknowledge that the old craftsmen's rules of the slow attainment of mastery must be significantly altered in his case, if not discarded altogether.

And most were glad to do so. To watch the boy work brought joy to every heart. His concentration was immense, almost unnaturally so. When given a task, regardless of how menial, he would lock onto the assignment, and not let go until it was completed. Food, the time of day, the weather - nothing seemed to deter him.

Good fortune had shined on him again when he was employed at the Brown shipyard. Theirs was one of the best shipyards in New York. The principals were convinced that they could build the very best ships in the world, ships unsurpassed in design, speed and elegant beauty. In very fact, this had already come to be, though the great seafaring nations of the world - England, Portugal, Spain, Denmark, Sweden - were loath to recognize this.

When he wasn't in the shipyard which was almost always Trask was on the wharves. He and his two friends - Aaron and Benjamin - went fishing, crabbing, and, every chance they got, sailing.

Trask and his young friends built the very first boat they sailed on - *Wharf Rat*. What a thrill for the boys to be sailing their own vessel among the greatest ships of the day. They saluted every ship that went by, and received salutes in return!

There are many reasons why a young man commits himself to a life on the sea; for some it's the possibility of riches; for others it's simply a job where no other seems suitable; for Trask, it was the challenge of it, to go fast and long and hard, against all that nature could send your way! There was no end to the challenge: if you're going fast, how can you go faster? If you're going long, how can you go longer? If you're going hard – how much can you take...

And once he had been smitten, he pursued sailing with the same single-minded intensity that he applied to everything. He read every chart and map in Brown's shipyard. He befriended captains and owners who came to check on the progress of their vessels, wearing them out with questions about the smallest details of their trade.

But, most of all, he sailed. When he conquered the challenge of sailing the East River, he sailed out to New York Harbor. When New York Harbor gave up its mysteries, he sailed out into the narrows.

On Trask's 19th birthday, one of Brown's clients needed

"someone cheap" to run lumber up from the Carolinas.

Like everyone else in Trask's life, Brown recognized the fire of destiny in the young man's face, and dared do nothing but enable its mission. Trask was unquenchable, irresistible, relentless, and overcame every obstacle like a weak ripple of a wave crushed by the plunging prow of a charging frigate under full sail.

William I. H. Trask

Though he would be losing a good hand, perhaps the best, Brown recognized the inevitability of his parting with Trask, and recommended him for the commission. Trask parlayed the successful completion of his first run into his next commission; then into another, and another.

With each voyage, Trask learned what no chart nor map nor prior captain could ever teach him. He acquired the kind of knowledge that doesn't reside in the head, or on a page; this knowledge seeped into his very skin, became incorporated in him. Only by breathing for months without relent the briny air that clangs in one's lungs like a fire bell, only by scoring one's skin rough and red and wrinkled with the unvarnished sun of the sea, only by searing into one's soul a permament rut that is the unbroken horizon, which bores into the eyes of a seamen, and takes up residence forever within his mind; only by knowing the utter negation of the sea at night, and the unmerciful boredom of the sea during the day, not from one night or one day, but from weeks and months and, yes, years, where the only means of holding onto one's concepts of time and space are the sextant, the chronometer, and a fevered compulsion to keep a conceptual framework imposed upon the world; only then can one say that the transformation has begun, from a creature of the land, to a creature of the sea.

And Trask's transformation had tempered his enthusiasm for risk-taking, as it should for all men of the sea. He had been sternly schooled in the mutability of life, and the constant abiding presence of disaster. When conditions are fair, only a naïve or foolish seaman would ever celebrate; when conditions are foul, they hold fast to the notion that it too will pass, and the fair weather return again.

And right now, aboard the ice-bound hulk of the *Young America*, Trask took to reminding himself that this storm will not last forever, and that if they could only get past the Verranzano Narrows into New York Harbor, everyone would be safe: himself, his first mate Conklin, the engineer Hammerschmidt, the cook Arnold, Kirkbak, Dunleavy, the passengers and the deck hands, including his 14-year-old son, Third Mate Joshua Trask.

Even those rare men who have been schooled through a lifetime on the water, who know what a rippling surface might mean, a patch of gray, still water in the midst of motion, seagulls circling overhead, clouds forming in the sky or a kiss from the wind, even those men, at night, are at the mercy of unseen forces, the wind, the tide, and the tendency of most things to sink in water...

Chapter Three

The Mooncussers

"I don't like it, Eck. Picking up boxes on the beach is one thing. I'll even row out to a ship that's already grounded. But a man's got to draw the line somewhere. Here's where I draw the line. It doesn't feel right."

Frank Eck walked in from the deck of his houseboat, *Sister Vincent*, with a blue claw crab in each hand. He plopped them both in a pot perched next to the iron stove.

"You're right, of course, Butler," Eck began. "If it doesn't feel right, you shouldn't do it. Whiskey?" Supercargo Butler shakes his head *no*. Joe the Indian nods his head *yes*. Eck pours one for himself and Butler anyway, and ignores Joe's request.

Eck opened the door to the stove, and stirred the wood embers, glowing orange and eager to heat within the stove.

"Let me ask you something, Butler," Eck began. "Does it *feel* right to be living in a one-room shack without a pot to piss in? Does it *feel* right to watch all the fine and fancy ladies go strolling right past your house? When the only reason they'll even look at you is to pity your sorry hide!!"

Even Joe the Indian winced.

"How do you think those fine and fancy ladies get to walking like this?" Eck stood up, and swayed his hips back and forth, mimicking a woman's walk. Puddin', the 12-year-old boy who had nowhere else to stay but on Eck's houseboat, giggled. "Do you think THEY worked for it? For Christ's sake, Butler, the old man wrung it out of your hide down in Carolina, stole it from the Indian, tricked the Chinaman, and do you think they give a good goddamn about *your* black behind?"

The orange light from the fire danced all around Supercargo Butler's eyes, now opened wider. Butler never liked coming to Eck's houseboat. It was too small, and Eck was too good, always talking him into something. Eck reminded him of a preacher, always driving him with words into somewhere he didn't want to be. Somehow he always came away thinking that maybe, just maybe, Eck was right. The world *wasn't* fair. There *was* a group of people somewhere in New York who were controlling everything. It wasn't right that they should have so much, and he so little, was it? Eck pressed his advantage.

"They kick you in the teeth, and you're smiling, thank you. No sir, not me. It's open season out there, and we're going hunting. Right boys?"

Joe the Indian nodded his lolling head, swimming in whiskey.

A cloud passed across Butler's face.

"Besides it's just this once, Butler," Eck consoled him. "We'll make a bloody fortune, if we do it right. More money than you can spend in four lifetimes, and that's it. We're gone. We'll blow off this beach like a leaf in a windstorm. No one will be the wiser, and we'll be richer than Midas.

"Besides, you've *got* to help us, Butler. You've got the boat."

Eck picked a live crab from a bucket, and tossed it at one of his cats. The cat squealed in rage as the crab clamped hard onto the cat's whiskers with his claw. Eck cackled with glee. Puddin' giggled uncontrollably.

"OK, but I won't kill anyone," Butler says, barely audible.

"The storm will do that, my friend. The storm will take care of everything.

"Here's the plan," Eck began as he unfolded a shipping document. "I have a friend in Grinnell's shop, a clerk, and they've a ship coming from China loaded with tea and spices - as good as gold - and I hear Miniturn is running one full of rum, a whole shipload of rum! Imagine that, chief. What would your people pay for a shipload of rum!"

Joe the Indian looked out of his watery eyes, and tried with effort to nod his head in agreement.

"Look at this barometer! Twenty-eight, and falling through the floor. There's more to this storm coming, I'm telling you. And when it does, we'll be ready. Butler, you're going to have to get your boat, bring it around tonight from the bay side, and meet us here. If we wait even an hour it may be too late."

FIRE ISLAND

Chapter Four

Young America

Trask locked eyes with his son, Joshua. He searched the boy's eyes to see how his play at confidence-building was going over with the crew. He could trust Joshua's eyes. There, he could read panic or trust, and everything in-between in an instant. What he read instead was something closer to blind faith. It seemed to say, 'Father had brought us this far; he'll bring us into port.'

Of all the looks Trask could have recorded at that moment - *that* was probably the scariest.

His other impression during that brief moment was how big Josh had grown. The clothes in which he had started the trip some eight months earlier looked ludicrous. It was as if his body had been stretched. He was thin and taut and strong like the lines he worked on the sails.

But there was something else in the boy's eyes, sadness - that damned sadness - that never went away even when he smiled. It was as if there was a part of the boy's heart that had been carved away that would never grow back, a missing piece.

Everyone could sense it, and woman of all ages lurched forward to fill that gap. Trask had seen this phenomenal reaction to his son time and time again. Yet Josh seemed non-plussed by the female attention; it was as if he was duty-bound to stand guard by his own wound, a wound that he was learning over time could never be healed.

It was his mother, of course. She was the wound, the missing piece, the part of his heart that would never be. She died two days after Josh's birth of Bright's disease, a kidney ailment that had been masked by her pregnancy. Throughout her pregnancy, she suffered severe back pain, vomiting and fever, but her mother and sisters, who cared for her at this time, had dismissed these as expected parts of the ordeal of childbirth.

Trask had been at sea at the time, and didn't learn of this until he returned to America some three months later. When he visited the infant, his care had already been commended to his aunt and grandmother, who were happy to take on the charge of this motherless boy, whom they named Joshua. Trask's only *proviso* was that he would return for Josh on his 10th birthday, and take him away to sea.

Trask then returned immediately to his vessel, the *Ambition*, and for the next 10 years never spoke his wife's name - Rebecca - again.

Trask had warned Rebecca about himself; he told her again and again what it would be like to be married to a captain; he described the long absences; he pointed out the death notices in the newspaper of sailors who never returned.

But she persisted in her devotion, beyond all reasons and all seasons. She would greet him at the wharves when he returned; she would offer him his first meal back home; she would see him off when he left again. She rejected all other suitors. She wanted him. Even if he didn't want her, she told him, she wanted *him*. And she meant it.

"My girlfriends and I would sneak of peek of you and your friends when you worked at Brown's," she once said. "I remember seeing you one day when you didn't think anyone was around. You sat down on a log. You were looking at the sun on the water. The wind was blowing your hair back away from your face. Then you cupped your hands together, and blew into them like a whistle. The sound I heard...I never expected that kind of sound to come from you, slow and mournful. It made me think of Joshua's trumpets at Jericho. The seagulls started coming around

- calling back in response, I fancied. After a bit, you got up, and walked back to your work.

"That day was a powerful tonic for me, William, and I can't shake it no matter how hard I try."

"Let's run her into shore."

Rebecca's constancy had a magnetic effect on him. She was like the North Star, always there in the same place in the sky, an unchanging point of reference, around which he traveled. At the end of one trip to Shanghai, he brought her back a necklace with a silver star pendant affixed with a cut diamond at its core.

They were married and Josh was conceived on their wedding night...

"Let's run her into shore," the captain shouted.

This was a tried and true tactic in a storm. Run the vessel parallel to the beach just outside the breakers. In so doing, Trask will use Fire Island, and Long Island behind it, as a kind of wind buffer. In this way, the people on-board are also closer to safety if the vessel goes down.

The *Young America* was now busting at about 13 knots, maximum hull speed. At this rate, they'd be through the Narrows leading into the harbor in about three hours. The eight-month trip had come down to this, the final three hours. Just get it through the Narrows, and we'll be safe, Trask thought...

"That's close enough," he shouted. The ship plowed along just outside the breakers. The captain knew there were no hidden shoals here, no rock outcroppings, just smooth sand underneath.

"Hammerschmidt?"

"Wind's steady at 20 knots now, gusts to 40. Still manageable, but they won't be getting lighter anytime soon. Barometer still falling."

"Strike the topsails, and the jib topsails. With this wind, we won't be needing them. Double-reef the main mizzen and spanker sails!"

"Lay aloft there, Trask, and furl that main-royal," the mate commanded the captain's son.

Trask went aloft, in a hurry, but he found it a mess. The braces had been let go, and the sail had entirely blown over to leeward. The sky-sail was adrift, and flapping wildly in the wind. Looking down, the young Trask saw little help for his plight, only confusion, and the hulk of the *Young America* tearing through the water with abandon. The masts were over at an angle of some 45 degrees to vertical. He saw his father pacing the deck, barking orders.

Everything topside was covered in ice. Despite the howling of the wind, and the hammering of the surf upon the hull, the most prominent sound was the crack and cackle of the rigging encased in ice.

Josh used the back end of an axe-head to shatter the ice from the lines. But his hands were wet and cold, such that he couldn't manipulate the lines. The pain in his hands was unbearable and, after a short time, he cried out, "I can't get the lines free!"

"Joshua! Get those sails furled!" his father re-commanded.

Wave after angry wave crashed over the gunwale, the upper railing of the ship, and, as they did, the rain fell in waves as well. The wind blew off the waves' white tops into sideways white wisps that joined to permeate the air with water.

Indeed, it became hard to distinguish the water from the air. Everything seemed to meld into one general wicked wetness. The world became a single color: gray - sky, sea, foam, waves. Gray.

The men's boots had long since filled with seawater, and their oilskins clung to them like a second skin. The crew had now been subjected to three days and nights of bitter exposure to the elements with little or no sleep.

Working might and main for an hour, the crew had double-reefed the top sails and the storm-sails.

"Hammerschmidt! Lash yourself to the wheel! Joshua, leave your perch, and report to the deck. Keep that forward cabin secure!"

They had done all they could with the sails. Steady on, at this point, and hope for the best.

Trask knew the *Young America* to be a good ship, not a great one. Having sailed her for eight months, he knew her idiosyncrasies well. She was a bit wide abeam, boxy and not very fast. She sailed low in the water, lower still now with her hull full of tea. Despite her low sailing profile, she tended to skip sideways across the surface and didn't take direction very well.

Yet despite these shortcomings, Trask knew her to be a brute strong plodder. Under the circumstances, he was glad to have her under him rather than many of the commissions he'd had in his time.

As night approached, the captain's great hope was that the mercury would fall enough to turn this hellish rain into snow. This would create other problems, he knew, but anything, at this point seemed to be an improvement over this relentless battering by the rain.

And the temperature *was* dropping, fast.

Soon, after sunset, the pelting rain began to sear the men's skin pummeling it like thin shards of glass. Ice now encased everything topside. The vessel became totally unmanageable. The running gear was frozen, and her sails were stiff with ice.

The *Young America* was a drifting iceberg.

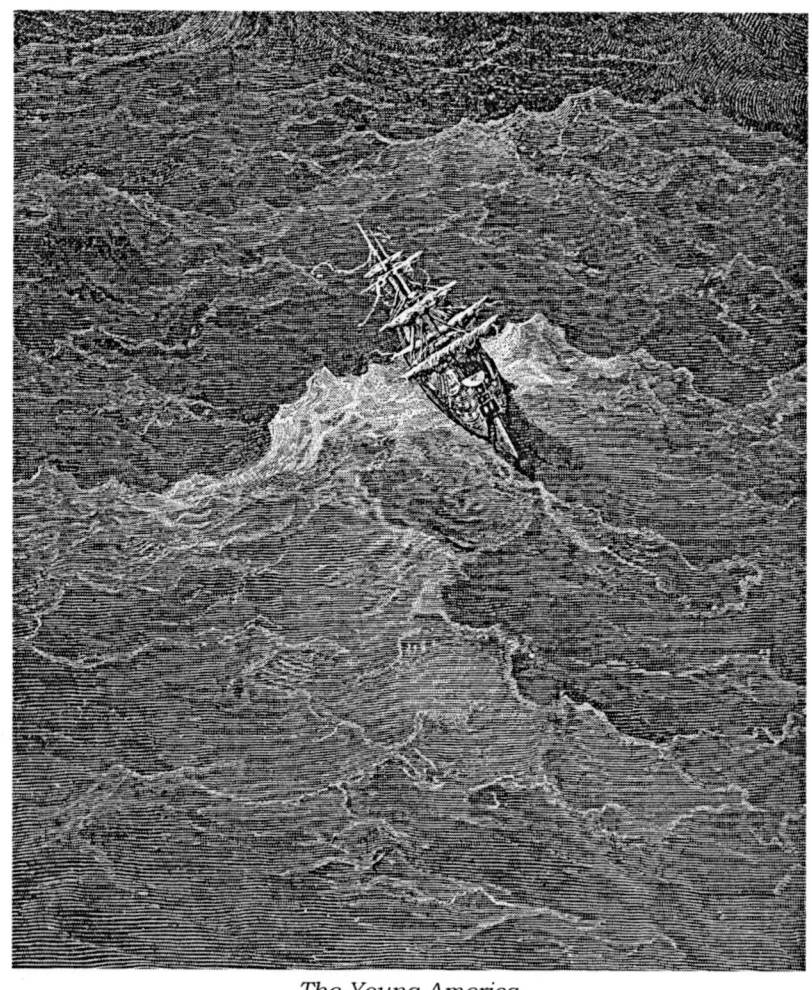

The Young America

Chapter Five

The Wreckmasters

Frank Eck struck a match against the rough rubber outer skin of his foul weather gear.
"Damn my eyes. Too wet! Gimme the lantern..."
Eck reached out for the whale oil lantern hanging off the side of Butler's mule. The light passing through the thick green glass momentarily cast a sickening hue on Eck's skin as he pushed the cigar stuck in his teeth toward the flame inside.

He drew in a few loving puffs as the flame danced wildly on the lit end of his cigar. Eck withdrew the cigar from this mouth, hitched his pants, and looked off toward the ocean.

"Won't be long now boys."

"I'm freezing."

"You're always cold, Butler. It's your African blood, too thin. And stop blocking the light! How's the damn crew going to see it if you're standing in front of it?"

Eck held the spyglass to his eye, and pointed it into the teeth of the wind and rain.

"Butler, I told you. I told you, dammit! *Here it comes!*"

In the darkness, Eck saw the red running lights of the *Young America* reflecting off its mainsail. Red lights, starboard side. The *Young America* was heading west.

With a green light on the seaward side of the mule, the crew of the *Young America* might mistake it for a vessel, and steer perilously close to shore.

"Is it coming closer?"

"It's hard to tell right now. It's so hard to see." Eck wiped the lens of the spyglass on his pants.

"Keep the mule going, Butler, nice and steady."

Eck stopped again to look. As he watched the approach of the *Young America*, he started singing to himself, a sea shanty.

> *What's the life of a man, any more than the leaves?.*
> *A man has his seasons, so why should we grieve?*
> *Although in this world, we appear bright and gay*
> *Like a leaf we must whither, and soon fade away.*

The relentless rain hammered the lens. A good wipe would yield about ten seconds of visibility.

"There she is, Butler. By god, there she is!..." But Butler and the mule were already well down the beach, as he had instructed.

"Here kitty, kitty, kitty..." Eck whispered to himself. "Here, kitty, kitty, kitty..."

Chapter Six

Lost at Sea

"How far from land?"
"Can't nearly tell, captain."

Trask peered through the driving rain. It was impenetrable now, though he thought he saw some lights. He shielded his eyes with his hands, and looked again.

"Hammerschmidt, are those ship lights to starboard?"
"Where do you see them, sir?"
"Two o'clock to starboard."

Hammerschmidt peered into the gray slush.
"I believe it is, sir?"

This confirmation provided an important clue to Trask's navigational reckoning. If there was a ship to starboard, that is, between his ship and shore, that meant there was plenty of water underneath his vessel.

"Drop the blue pigeon," Trask said, ordering a sounding.
"Twenty-six fathoms."

Looking again toward the lights, Trask estimated that the ship was at least 600 yards to leeward. He tried the spyglass, but found it utterly useless in this rain. Indeed, it provided poorer visibility than his unaided eye.

He continued his tack toward shore, somewhere well astern of the accompanying vessel.

The intensity of the storm continued to increase. It peaked to a steady howl, and relentlessly maintained that intensity. Trask felt the vessel pitch over a massive wall of water, and into the hollow of the storm's mercy. In the trough of water, the *Young America* hit bottom. There was no mistaking it, that dull grinding thud of a 90-ton vessel scraping along sand and small stone. The impact was brief as the next upwelling of water raised the vessel up and off the sand, but the implication was profound.

"Bottom here?!" By Trask's reckoning, they were still a good 1/2 mile from shore. Had he misinterpreted the sound?

"Hammerschmidt?!"

"That would be bottom, sir."

"Take another sounding."

"Two fathoms." It must be the sand bar, Trask thought, lying parallel to the beach about a quarter of a mile off shore.

"Hard to port, Hammerschmidt!"

Hammerchmidt muscled the wheel. "The gear is frozen, sir."

"Unfreeze it, dammit!"

The wave action made merry of the crew's designs. As a massive roil of water passed underneath the vessel, the rudder itself was lifted clean out of the water. Trask issued another order.

"Let go starboard anchor!" It seemed the only chance now to stay off the bottom.

"Cut the halyards!" Trask hoped this would release the sails, but it was impossible to do so; they were so heavily encased in ice. The ice draped over the lines like blobs of candlewax clinging to the side of a well-burnt candle.

His commands were coming fast and furious now, but working the vessel was impossible. After about 30 fathoms had run out, the anchor chain parted.

The wind was now blowing them inexorably toward shore.

"There's a chance we could make it through the Fire Island inlet!" Hammerschmidt said.

"A slim chance, Hammerschmidt. In this weather there's no seeing it."

The waves and the wind drove the vessel toward shallower and shallower water. The hull scraped bottom again, this time seeming to dig itself into the soft sand like a crab burrowing for safety from the storm. They were 500 yards from shore.

A massive tonnage of water approached from the port side, and slapped the vessel silly. It was enough to spin the vessel off its sandy perch. The boat was listing badly now toward shore.

"Send up a distress flare. Issue one every five minutes."

Josh Trask fumbled for a few minutes with the device. Finally it fizzled out on the deck, a victim of the moisture.

"Throw everything overboard that isn't secure to the vessel."

In the trough of another monster wave, the *Young America* put down hard. The jolt cracked timbers in the hull.

"Drop the port anchor!" Trask yelled. With the tide going out, he figured he could spin the vessel around.

"We're taking on water, captain!"

"Hammerschmidt, man the pump! All hands, throw all non-essentials overboard!"

The vessel was listing 30 degrees to starboard, and the waves were making cruel work of the *Young America*. The stout bulwarks, hewn from the strongest timbers, were torn from their fastenings. Iron bolts were bent and twisted. Deck structures had been pulverized to splinters. Cordage on-deck, fallen from the spars, made passageway an adventure, and the sea around the vessel was a boiling stew of destruction and debris, stark evidence of the destruction of the *Young America*.

After 1/2 hour of pumping water, and lightening the vessel through disposal, the ship was only closer to disintegration. Even if they could float the vessel off the bottom, it would surely sink. Indeed, now the bottom seemed an ally preventing the broken vessel to which the crew hung like barnacles from being swallowed by the hard sea.

The crew seemed at a loss.

"Let's swim for it." Conklin yelled.

"Swim for it, and you're' a dead man," Trask growled.

"Stay on this ship, and I'm a dead man!"

"We need you on the ship, and help is coming."

"Go down with this ship if you must captain, but I believe we can make it."

Conklin grabbed a life ring, and jumped overboard into the frigid tumult. Immediately a wave overwhelmed him, and he bobbed up on the back side of it gasping for air. His breathing was short, fast and shallow - hyperventilation - brought on by the sudden shock of the ice-cold water to his body. He was traveling fast along the leeward side of the vessel.

"Throw him a line," Trask commanded. This is done, but Conklin ignores it as he flails his arms in a frantic and hopeless battle against the powerful current running along the shore.

"Again, another line, quickly." Trask calls out. This toss falls well short. It is clear that Conklin is not approaching closer to shore, but away from it. He dips, once more, behind the swelling mass of a monster wave, and is not seen again.

Chapter Seven

Fire In the Sky

On the beach, the deaf-mute, Murray, rustles around in his bedraggled equipment shed on the beach. Murray is polishing a brass candle lamp that obviously needs a lot of polishing. He could use a little polish, too. He has no front teeth, and his curly hair sticks out from underneath a dirty wool cap.

Rummy, a dog of uncertain lineage, stares up at him with doleful eyes from his spot on the floor, obviously his best friend.

Murray puts the candle lamp aside, and turns to preparing his bed for the night when he sees the flare.

Murray's eyes are agog, his mouth opens and closes involuntarily as the mangled sounds of a soul in crisis wrestle their way through the taut muscles of his throat.

"MMyow! Mmyow! Mmy eeeeee..." A shrill scream issues from his mouth like a 2-year-old child being terrorized by an older brother.

Murray lurches through the opening of his lean-to to the fire pit outside, and grabs two pans which he bangs frantically together in a frightening fury.

He starts running down the beach. The sand is heavy and wet, and makes for tough-going, but Murray is frantic, flailing his arms wildly to each side. Rummy is running beside him, his tongue lolling out one side of his mouth.

"Mmm-yow!"

The ghastly crimson glow from the lit flare casts long weird shadows onto the wet sand. Murray's leaden footfalls follow the beachhead as it winds its way around to the left. He stumbles, driving his left shoulder hard into the sand. Looking up from where he has fallen, he sees a recognizable cut in the dune grass.

His chest heaving, gasping for air, he continues to push himself in an ungainly walk-run up the beach through the cut in the dune grass to the doorway of a house.

"Mm-yow! Yow!" Murray frantically bangs on the door with the palms of his hands.

A candle glow appears in one of the windows, and works its way through the house downstairs to the front door, which opens, and reveals the candlelit face of Cassandra Wolff, the President of the New Hope Relief Society.

Cassandra looks at Murray's face, sees a red flare dying out over the breakers, and knows in an instant why he has come to her door.

She runs around to the back of the house, and begins to ring the alarm bell with vigor. She hands to rope to Murray, and gestures to him to keep ringing. Cassandra goes inside the house where she is immediately encountered by Dahlia, her live-in maid and assistant.

"M's Wolff, what's the matter?"

"Ship ashore. Get the gear."

Chapter Eight

Fire and Ice

The enormity of the accelerating peril is now evident to Trask. Nothing has prepared him for this. Not his work in the shipyard, not his many years sailing the world. He had never lost a ship out from underneath him. Somehow he had always managed to scramble at the last minute, pull the rabbit from the hat, avert disaster. His greatest strength had always been a mindset focused stone-cold on a positive outcome. When everyone around him had already given up, Trask had continued to seek options, trying a completely fresh tack, if necessary, to solve a seemingly unsolvable problem.

But *this*! Now he was out of options, now it wasn't just the possibility of defeat, but defeat itself staring him in the face. He was not trained to cope with this, because in training for defeat, you invite it, you learn to expect it. He never had to make decisions as a defeated man.

But the empirical evidence presented by one's senses can sometimes crash through even the most impregnable of hardened fortresses, a lifetime of training in victory.

Thinking thus, he watched Joshua scramble across the deck like a wet spider. Suddenly, there was a wrenching snap from above as one of the spars collapsed. As it awkwardly tumbled down through what was left of the rigging, it cut through a line holding a boom in position. The massive boom began careening in a sweeping arc across the deck.

"Swinging boom! Joshua, look out! Joshua!!!" The boom caught up the boy along with other debris littering the deck, and flung him like a sack of flour to starboard. He was entangled awkwardly in the rudder chains hanging over the side, obviously in pain, half in the water, half out.

"Dad!"

Trask had already scrambled from his perch to save him, but just as he reached for the boy a huge wave crested up, and slammed into the side of the ship, knocking Trask forward. Righting himself, he peered through the thick rain toward his son. But the light had failed from the last flare, and he saw nothing.

"Joshua!"

"Joshua!"

A sharp schism of horror, like of lightening bolt, tore through his gut. Trask scrambled across the deck over broken spars, and a tangled morass of lines that blocked his way. When he finally approached the starboard side of the deck, all he saw was emptiness.

He looked out on the roiling waves for a sign of him. The sea looked back - gray, like rancid meat, marbleized with frothy veins of foam. Trask scanned the boiling mass acutely.

"Joshua! Joshua!" Gone.

If he jumped in now, he would surely die in a futile effort to find his lost son. If he stayed with the boat, he might live, yet live forever with the image of his poor boy being swallowed by an angry sea, reaching out to cling to life, wild fear his last emotion. Trask paused like a ship teetering on the precipice of a huge wave, suspended between two valleys, both deep and forbidding. He looked hard and long into the tumult.

Is it better to die now, than to fight for a life that will be doomed by the hauntings of that final image of his son?

Just then, another spar collapsed from overhead, and Trask leapt sideways to avoid the falling debris. This instinctual response to danger snapped Trask back to the world. He saw two silhouettes on the port side.

"Wrap yourself in all the clothing you can!" came Trask's ominous orders.

Trask went down below, and scrambled for some blankets in his cabin. He found them in a locker under some debris. He opened the top drawer of his desk, and pulled out the captain's log of the ship's voyage. The water in his quarters was now ankle deep. Topside, the rain has since turned to hail and sleet. For a moment, the sound of it pelting the ship captured his attention. Suddenly, Trask became aware of his surroundings in the cabin, acutely aware. Personal items were strewn without heed by the tossing ship; all those things cared for, tended to, during the voyage were not needed now. There was quiet here in the cabin amidst the mayhem on deck. Mortality had come to sit for a while like an overweight guest who lingers at tea.

Trask was tempted to linger with Him, but a thought roused him from his trance. He scrambled out the cabin door, to the quarters Josh shared with the other deckhand. It was a cramped space with little room for more than two hammocks and small chest of drawers.

Trask rifled through the clothes neatly stowed in the drawers as the boy had been commanded to do, and found a tidy red book in which Josh had kept his own log of this voyage. This, he stuffed into his coat alongside the official ship's log. Just then, Trask lurched forward striking his forehead on a beam. The ship had shifted again, rather suddenly.

Trask worked his way up the gangway topside, and was struck by the scene of misery on deck. The *Young America*, its keel now firmly buried in the yielding sand on the bottom, was now listing badly to starboard. Indeed, a good third of the deck was now completely submerged.

There was clearly no hope of floating this vessel off the sand in any tide. The spars and the shrouds formed a tangled mass of debris upon the deck. To traverse the deck was nearly impossible, the angle of the deck being so steep, and the obstacles so many.

One of the masts was intact, though stripped of most of the sail and attached booms and lines. The aft mast was perhaps two thirds its original height, the top third having crashed down upon the deck.

Just as Trask's mind grasped the full reckoning of the mayhem, the vessel was smashed by another massive wave, full on. The *Young America* groaned, and parts of her snapped. It was a killer blow, and caused her to list even further.

Arnold, the cook, had gathered what remained of the ship's crew and passengers on deck.

"May the Fates be kind to us all," he offered, as he took the first slug from the bottle of whiskey. He wiped off his mouth with the back of his hand, and passed the bottle around…

"May the Fates be kind to us all."

Chapter Nine

Beach Pirates

"Why don't we just wait, Eck? The surf will smash that boat to pieces by morning, and we'll have all the loot we want, right on shore."

A self-imposed lethargy has descended upon Supercargo Butler as he limply wrestled with the heavy wet canvas sail that covered his boat.

"The buzzard beachcombers will get it all!" Eck hissed. "Look, haven't I gotten us this far? Didn't I tell you this ship was coming? Didn't my idea with the lanterns work? *This is it*! *Tonight*! Do you realize what is on that ship, Butler?"

"Yeah, stiffs," he replied dolefully.

"Hong Kong tea, maybe 500 cases. Do you know what people will pay for *one* case of that stuff?"

"I'm not going to kill anybody, Eck. If someone is on that boat, I'm not going to kill them. You can go on. I'll stay in the boat."

"Butler, believe me, there's nobody alive on that vessel. By the time we get there, they'll all be stiffs. So the tea is fair game. It's the law of the sea. First come, first served. And right now, it's time to serve tea!"

Eck's goofy grin followed the remark revealing more gaps than teeth.

With the canvas tarp off, the three men lugged the wretched boat down the sandy slope toward the surf. It lurched forward like an oversized turtle done with its egg-laying.

"Ease it in, gentlemen," Eck cautioned. "*Ease* it in."

But Butler and Joe the Indian were panting like dogs on a hot afternoon. Problem was, it was seven degrees Fahrenheit above zero.

"Eck you're crazy!" Butler screamed above the roar. "Look at those waves!"

Joe the Indian moaned. The temples of his head were throbbing so hard it felt like his brain was trying to get out.

"It's now or never men," Eck commanded as he positioned himself behind the rickety vessel. "On the count of three - one, two, THREE!!!"

Using the gunwale as leverage, Joe the Indian lifted himself up out of the water, and into the boat like a gymnast. Eck was flopping off the stern like a stuck fish, half in the water, half in the boat, balanced by his stomach on the transom, and desperately trying to throw his weight forward. Butler was now in water up to his chest, hopelessly immersed in the churning surf.

"Joe, pull me in!" Eck screamed.

As Joe moved to do so, the boat tipped shoreward, and a massive wave lifted the teetering vessel precariously into the air. For a brief horrifying moment, Eck looked down, and saw the landing area for his boat and crew. The water was rushing down the slope of the beach, and into the foot of the wave like the plug had been pulled on the ocean. A hollow sucking sound echoed into the curl of the wave. At this rate of return, there was a chance there would be no water to land on at all!

In the grip of the monster's maw, there was nothing Eck could do but fall, fall with his boat, fall with Joe the Indian, fall with Butler (though God knew where he was), fall with his grand scheme, fall, if he was lucky, into four inches of rapidly receding water, to be followed by tons of angry, agitated, ice-encrusted ocean...

Chapter Ten

Up The Masts

"Men, bring up three cases of tea from below," Trask ordered. "Tie a line to each, and throw them overboard. Maybe they'll reach the shore, and us with them."

But the cases got caught up in the lines clinging to the vessel all around like a desperate jellyfish. Trask was not about to wait for the cases to work themselves free.

"To the riggings for your lives men!" Trask yelled while handing a soggy blanket to each man.

"Wrap yourselves in this, and up the mast."

"We'll freeze up there!" Arnold complained.

"We'll drown down here a lot sooner."

Trask began scaling the mizzen-mast so that a line could be tied off at the first cross spar. The masts were coated with a half-inch thick sheen of ice, dabbled with pointy pricks whipped up by the wind wrapping itself around the massive wooden cylinders. As Trask's gloved hand reached for the mast, tiny glasslike shards of ice break off, and fly toward the swamped deck below. Brittle and slick, the masts are unmercifully difficult to hold onto, particularly in a 45-knot gale.

Trask manages to latch one hand on a crossing spar which he uses as leverage for a final pull of his body weight.

Now, with the cross spar under his crotch, he ties off one end of the line he had carried with him, and drops the other to the deck below.

Dunleavy went next. The swaying of vessel made his climb up the rope agonizingly slow to watch. Each time the ship swayed, he would lose his footing on the mast, and twist in the line for a time before he could right himself again. At one point, the ship shifted, increasing the angle of its list toward the shore. When the line swayed off the mast this time, Dunleavy lost his grip, and plummeted headlong into the surf without uttering a sound.

For those remaining on deck, this was an awful scene because they now had to climb that same line. But given that the deck was now almost completely awash, they had no choice.

For Trask, this was surreal - 30 feet above the washed out deck of his vessel in a storm of such fury watching his two remaining shipmates climbing up an uncertain line toward him. His hands felt as though they would break off at the arms, they were so cold.

And then he began to think of Josh. At first, he tried to shrug off the image. His son, helpless in the hand of God, locking into those eyes. 'Dad!' His son never called him *Dad*. Trask couldn't remember another time that he did. Then, water...gone. Washed off the face of the earth.

Trask became suddenly afraid to look down into the surf, afraid he might see his boy's lifeless body. He sagged back into the cross of the spars, and stared into the storm with ice encrusting even the lashes of his weary eyes.

Is it me, he thought. Rebecca, Joshua, his crew, his ship... *Is it me?*

"Trask!"

It was Arnold holding on for his life to the rope, twisting helplessly some 20 feet over the roiling surf slashing its way over the deck.

"Trask! Help!"

Trask grabbed the line, and began hauling it up. The weight on it seemed immense. Arnold was over 220 pounds, swinging on an untethered line caked with ice. If only Trask had better leverage, he could master the task, but he was sitting astride an icy spar 30 feet in the air. His numb hands worked as if by themselves, separate from the frenzied commands given them by his overworked mind.

"Hurry Trask! I can't hold on."

"Wrap your ankle in the line!" Trask shouted.

"I can't!" Arnold cried out. He was sobbing now like a three-year-old. "I c-a-a-an't!"

"Try it! Now! It will keep you from falling!"

"I can't do it. Pull me up!"

Trask located a stud on the mast to tie off the slack as he pulled. He managed to stand, using the mast for support. His greatest challenge now was a sickening sense of vertigo that overcame him as he looked down the long straight line that led directly to his death. Was he pulling the line up? Or was it pulling him down?

For his part, Arnold, still blubbering like a baby, clung to the rope like an infant to his mother.

"Arnold, reach up; you can grab the spar now."

"New...new...new..." He repeated over and over like a kitten too scared to come in out of the rain.

"Arnold, get control of yourself, man. *Grab the spar!*"

"New...new..."

Exasperated, Trask tied off the line, grabbed Arnold, and hoisted him by the petard onto the frozen spar.

The effort depleted Trask, and for many minutes he laid, chest heaving, with his face in the crotch of his arm. As he did so, he felt the ice forming a thin white sheet all around his body like a comforting shroud...

FIRE ISLAND

Chapter Eleven

On the Beach

Cassandra Wolff stood on the peak of the tallest sand dune, her arms akimbo. On one side of her was Murray; on the other, Dahlia, her assistant. On her shoulder was the strap of a large canvas bag that weighed some 30 pounds. Inside the bag were gauze, cloth, a bottle of chloroform, a bottle of whisky, a blanket, a sharp knife, tweezers, a thick book called *Diagnosis and Treatment of Common Maladies*, and a canvas and wood rig she could assemble as a stretcher. On her head was a wide-brimmed canvas cap that cast a shadow across her eyes, shadows caused by the fresh bonfire roaring on the beach.

As Cassandra Wolff strode down from the dunes, she walked through the gathering of townspeople on the beach, helpless. Most had come via sleighs drawn by horses, and had made the trip over the frozen bay between Fire Island and the mainland in little more than an hour.

Some had followed the spirit of adventure to be here, some had a true desire to help. Some had come for the treasures they might find washed up along the beach, beachcombers.

"Can't we do anything?" Cassandra asked no one in particular. "Are we to just stand here while they die?"

"Even with a boat, ma'am, we're ill-prepared to launch it," one of the men piped up. "What with this surf, the boatmen would be dead, too, in a hurry."

"And besides," he said after a moment's reflection, "we don't have a boat. Kerrigan's is the nearest one, and they've already gone to fetch it."

"What about the boy's ice scooter?" Cassandra suggested. Hearing this, the two boys on the beach looked at each other like they had just won a sweepstakes.

"Ma'am, have you actually *seen* that scooter sail?" the man asked quizzically.

"Well, why not? These boys here came across the bay on it."

"It sails on water, too," Peter, one of the boys, chimed in.

The two boys had traversed the bay in an ice-scooter, an eight-foot polished wood oblong furnished with a mast and two sails, that, with a decent wind would skip across the frozen surface of the bay. There was more than a decent wind *this* night.

The sea was a grinding mass of ice porridge two feet deep, and dotted with huge blocks of snarling ice. The breakers, 20 feet tall, flung this chaotic sluice up onto the surfline with each successive lunge, piling cakes of ice that were as high as eight feet.

"Men like you ought to be able to reach that stranded vessel. It's right there. I can see it," she said pointing at the dark silhouette mortally wounded in the surf. As she did a huge wall of froth and fury rose up off the beach like a chilling crescendo to an orchestral movement. The force of it seem to move the very sand beneath their feet.

The life ring, taken when Conklin jumped overboard, had already washed up. Blankets covered two bodies laid out above the surfline.

One of the great challenges now was keeping the people on the beach through the night without freezing to death. Search parties were organized to scour the surrounding beach for firewood. Two people were appointed as keepers of the bonfire.

"What about a rope?" she countered. "A rope attached to a cannonball. We shoot the cannonball over the ship. The rope will then be accessible to the people on board. Then we haul them in."

"It's a notion, ma'am. And I know they've tried that very thing in England, with some success. But we don't have a cannon. Even if I knew where to get one, it would take forever to haul it along this sand. And, by then, those poor souls would be frozen stiff anyway."

"We've got to do *something*," Cassandra implored.

"We're doing more than something," the man said, looking up at her with sloe, heavy-lidded eyes. "We're doing everything we can. When Kerrigan's boat gets here, we'll launch the boat, and rescue whoever is left on-board. But that may not be 'til morning. In the meantime, these people have to be kept warm."

His words were delivered without rancor, and carried the force of reason. She could see he was right, but to admit it outright felt like surrender, and Cassandra Wolff did not surrender easily...

"It's right there. I can see it."

FIRE ISLAND

Chapter Twelve

Scuttle

"This is not the end, boys," Eck said to the black cast-iron stove squat in the middle of his ramshackle houseboat. "Oh, no. This is just the beginning, *just* the beginning..."

His two hands were clasped around a china cup filled with whiskey, a thick Indian blanket slumped around his shoulders.

"Those wreckmasters won't be beating me out of my tea. That tea is *ours* now. It's the law of the sea. Finders keepers."

"I'm cold, Eck," Butler moaned. "So cold."

"Throw another log on the fire, Joe. Our man here is *so cold*." Eck cast a wicked sideways glance at this large lump of a man.

"Butler, perhaps if you had actually gotten *in* the boat, instead of sloshing around in the water, you wouldn't be *so cold* now."

"I tried," Butler whimpered.

"Trying isn't good enough. Doing is good enough. And doing is what we are going to do in the morning."

Just as the sweet burn of another sip of whiskey echoed in his head, Eck launched into a familiar theme.

"You know that whiskey we're drinking right now, Joe? The best single malt whiskey in Scotland. Do you know where I got that? Off a ship! The *Spirit of England*! You know that warm wool blanket on your lap right now, Butler? Do you know where I got that? Off a ship! I got a case of them. For nothing. Free. I broke no laws, and nobody can claim them. Do you know how long I would have to work plucking potatoes to get that stuff?

Meanwhile, people like Grinnell and his cronies own half the bloody nation!"

Eck spit into the open door of the stove.

"Life is too short, and when you're dead, you're dead for a long, long time. I'm going to enjoy my living while I've got the chance, and our chance is here now, boys. Tea for the taking!"

He looked around the room for effect. "As long as we don't lose our nerve."

It was another winning tirade, and Eck knew just when to wind it up. It was hopeless arguing with him. So Butler resigned himself to the fact that they would launch the boat again in the morning, just four hours away at this point. Trying to sleep now would be pointless. Drinking more might help, but it would also make the pain greater in the morning.

"Four hours. By then the storm should let up. If you want to sleep, I got two cots in the back room. Otherwise you can sit around the campfire here, and listen to me play my Jew's Harp."

With that he took out a silver mouth harp from a hardwood case, clamped on it with his teeth, and began to *twang*. After a few preliminary plucks, he looked over at Butler slumped in misery and resignation.

"Got this off a boat, too," he said, gesturing to the small instrument in his hand, and cackled so wildly that he almost fell backwards off his perch.

Chapter Thirteen

The White Shroud

Trask felt as if he could sleep, despite the circumstances. Splayed out on a wooden spar 30 feet in the air, hovering over a churning storm-tossed sea, being pelted with icy rain and 40-knot gusts, his body yearned for the descent into the phantom world where the grinding logic of the material world is suspended. After three days and nights without sleep, his body was finally shutting down, taking a swan dive into the netherworld, whizzing through various levels of consciousness, like someone falling from a high place, plummeting headlong into unconsciousness.

Paranormal connections of random images began clicking away in his mind, the transition stage between wakefulness and sleep. Trask eased into this surreal world fascinated by the kaleidoscope of strange imagery. Then, like a roulette wheel whirring past, and then - *click, click* - finally stopping, the image of Josh's face and outstretched hand came up on the screen in Trask's mind. It jolted him to wakefulness again.

For a moment he lay on the spar assessing where, and who he was. He listened to the creaking of the ice-encrusted ship, felt the wicked sting of the salt air splintering his cheeks, thought about his shipmates.

For all he knew now, he could be the last person alive on the ship.

"Arnold!" he shouted weakly. "Arnold!"

Arnold was gone. Perhaps he had fallen. Trask looked down over the side of the spar, and saw not Arnold, but Kirkbak, hung in the rigging, head downward, held by the lashing he had placed around his ankle, frozen in the ratlines, swaying to and fro' in the pitiless gale.

He looked aft, and thought he saw a bundled silhouette in the crosstrees of the foremast. Could be Morrison. Dead?

"Morrison!" No reaction. "Morrison!"

Just then the red conflagration of another Coston flare on the beach caught Trask's eye. There is a bonfire on the beach, too! Though Trask had no way of signaling, these sights encouraged him immeasurably. Perhaps they can launch a boat. It may not be too late after all.

"Trask!"

Trask looked around, but could not find the source of the voice calling his name. For a moment, he thought he might not have heard it at all.

"Trask!" It was Arnold's voice, close by, but still he couldn't see him.

"I'm in here."

Trask saw a gloved hand waving from inside the furled mizzen top sail. The lashing had been cut, and Arnold had apparently climbed into the opening between the massive folds of the canvas.

Trask crawled down the mast on all fours, and entered Arnold's sanctuary.

"I thought you were dead," was Arnold's greeting.

"I thought *you* were dead," Trask returned.

The canvas cocoon cut the effect of the wind completely, but both men were soaked to the bone, and blue from exposure to the cold. Arnold was shivering uncontrollably.

"I think I saw Morrison on the foremast," Trask reported. "He may be alive."

"We may not be in the morning," Arnold replied without emotion.

Trask painfully removed his hands from his frozen gloves, and worked them underneath his oilskins for warmth. There was no sensation whatsoever in either hand.

Here he was, now faced with a long slow overnight vigil with, of all people – Arnold: a selfish, childish lump of a man.

More than once, Trask wished for death that terrible night, but his body would not obey its master. His heart pumped on, though slower; his mind spun in chaotic orbits like electrons that have lost their moorings, but spin on it did. Against his will, his body lived on through a night of excruciating pain, and boredom, waiting to die or live, his body programmed to function despite the protestations of his desperate mind.

Arnold's mind, on the other hand, was haunted by the image of a steaming cup of hot black coffee. If only he had *just that*, he thought time and again, this night could be tolerated. By his reckoning, he hadn't eaten in two days.

Trask's mind kept returning to Josh's face just before getting washed overboard. The image became exquisite and unbearable torture, far worse than the physical pains in his body.

After a time, he forced himself to think of something else. He fixed his mind on the Port of Shanghai, reconstructing every last possible detail: the noxious smell of the harbor, the overwhelming crowds on the dock, the courtly manner of Houqua, the Grand Merchant, over tea.

But, time and again, it came back to his son until, blessed relief, he slipped again into a shallow and fitful sleep.

FIRE ISLAND

Chapter Fourteen

The Vigil

The group of bystanders had grown to about two score, who busied themselves through the night searching for firewood, and tending to the bonfire that became the font of life for everyone on the beach, and a source of hope for those still alive on the stranded and broken vessel.

Three wave-lashed corpses had now washed ashore. These were fetched from the surf, and laid out in a neat row some 20 feet from the fire. No blankets were drawn over them; they being more useful to the living. What a ghastly array, a haunting vision of lifelessness on the icy beach, pale, motionless, with only the dancing shadows from the fire reflecting off the prone figures.

The body of young Josh was not among them.

Kerrigan's boat, *Soliloquy*, arrived just before daybreak, some 10 hours after the shipwreck was first spotted. A recalcitrant mule fixed to a makeshift carriage had pulled through the night with Kerrigan and his cousin, prodding and pushing and pleading the whole way.

The boat was a sorry sight, a boxy bulk of bulging hardwoods that Kerrigan had built himself. It was a crude hybrid, built both for sail and for oar that Kerrigan had fashioned for his needs on the bay side of Fire Island. He fished and crabbed in it, and could even drag a homemade dredge for clams.

But up against the ocean surf, in a Nor'east'r, it seemed overmatched, and the hearts grew heavy of those who kept this vigil on the beach.

"I would have been here a lot sooner, if I could have sailed her," Kerrigan announced sweetly. "But the surf wouldn't let me."

Kerrigan was one of the thinnest people you could imagine, and one of the oddest. But for his cousin, who usually helped him out during fishing season, he spent his days alone. He did everything, and built everything, himself. He was one of the few baymen who had built his house on the south side of the bay, on Fire Island. He built it with wood he found washed up on the beach.

His boat was occasionally employed in rescue efforts like this one because it was one of, perhaps, three on the entire length of the island that could be transported by carriage overland. It was understood the pick of the cargo would go home with him. In the case of the *Young America*, Kerrigan's boat was the closest, and, come hell or high water, it was the best and only chance to save whoever may be still alive on board.

The wives of two of the men from the mainland took their husbands aside, and pleaded for them not to get into that boat to attempt a rescue now. One woman could be heard saying, "There's no one left alive on that ship anyway."

By the look of the sorry vessel, it would be hard to argue with her logic - broken in half, stranded in the breakers, the blocks swaying aimlessly back and forth with the motion of the vessel, it was hard for those on the beach to believe the ship had *ever* been sea-worthy. She was a ghostly silhouette, a forlorn skeleton, all the life having gone out of her, the spirit of the ship having left her as surely as it had left each of the three bodies that lay prone on the beach beside the fire.

The sea itself was littered with great pieces of wreckage, strange uncanny lumps that later resolved themselves to be furniture or planks from the huge ship.

"You may be right," the man replied to his wife. "But *somebody* has to cut those men down from the rigging."

Chapter Fifteen

The Longest Night

"Trask," Arnold says, shivering. "I can't take it anymore. I'm going to swim ashore."

"Don't do it, Arnold. You'll be dead in three minutes."

"From what? The cold?" Arnold replied bitterly. "I can't feel anything on my body as it is! How can I get any colder, or wetter, than I am now! I'm already at the limit. We're just waiting to die, Trask. I can't take that. I've *got* to do something!"

Trask lowered his head trying to come up with a way to change Arnold's mind.

"I've been thinking about it," Arnold continued. "I'll tie a rope around my waist. That way, if I start to drown you can pull me in. If I make it, though, I'll pull *you* across all the way to the beach!"

It sounded like a good plan, compelling in its simplicity, an apparently fail-safe approach that could result in salvation. But even in his weakened state, Trask could see clearly that it was suicide. Years and years of practical problem-solving overruled the slim hope of Arnold's desperate gambit.

Yet, how to counter Arnold's obviously insane passion for this scheme?

Trask raised his head, and looked Arnold in the eye, something he had not done in the several hours in which they had shared the canvas shelter in the sky.

"Arnold, if you try that crazy idea, you will die. And if you die, I swear to you, I will kill myself. I have lost my son, my ship, and my entire crew, but you. If you go, the only thing I will have left is my knife." With that Trask unsheathed his knife, looking dull and deadly in the dim light of the canvas shroud, and held it to his neck.

Trask was shouting now at the top of his lungs, his rage at life surging through his body, supercharging it again with energy. Somehow, he had to stop the fierce momentum of death and destruction wrought by this storm. Somehow he had to stop this wicked undertow from sucking everything he once knew into the abyss. Even if it was only Arnold, a sorry coward of a man, even if it meant a promise to take his own life, so be it. Trask frightened even himself with the conviction behind his words.

"I will use it. God help you, Arnold, I *will* use it. I have nothing to lose."

The sound of Trask's voice died quickly when his peroration ended. As loud as it was, when it was gone the memory of it seemed small and silly next to the howling winds that continued unabated in its absence. His ice-encrusted face was contorted into a grotesque mask.

Arnold, shouted into submission, started crying again. First it came in tiny burblings that started in his throat, and finished with a self-conscious little sniff from his nose; then it escalated into jerky paroxysms of woe, still dammed in part by a paltry attempt at self-control; then the full force of his grief and self-pity poured through, unimpeded, into a full-throated wail. With his eyes awash in tears, and his head turned to the sky, Arnold reverted into a pitiful, blubbering child again.

Trask looked away, trying hard not to be reminded of Josh. As a small boy, Josh would collapse into similar fits. His spirit was like that of an all-powerful genie trapped in a bottle, a giant ambition contained in a little, growing body; an imagination that free-ranged the world, stuck in a frame that couldn't lift 70 pounds; eyes that could see to the horizon; feet, in shoes that protected him from the earth.

Occasionally, borne of this frustration, immense explosions of emotion would overcome the boy. He would surrender to it, and then emerge, purged, some time later, his eyes crisp and bright like the morning after an October storm.

This voyage on the *Young America*, his first trans-oceanic voyage, seemed to feed and mellow his gargantuan spirit. Finally the scope and challenge of the boy's life seemed equal to the aspirations of his heart. The movements of his lithe and muscular figure assumed a new grace, burnished by the blunt stern tool of experience. The long slow fuse of his destiny burned with the brightness of magnesium on that trip, and his father saw, for the first time, what kind of man he could become. He, like his father, seemed destined to become a leader of men. And, despite the colossal achievements of his father, Josh seemed sure to supercede them.

This gladdened his heart, but then...gone. Once here, then gone. Gone...

From within this reverie, Trask looked out toward the bonfire on shore. The significance of the nebulous shadows on the beach, momentarily revealed through a break in the rain, didn't register at first. Still his mind upheld the image of Josh, hovering like a radiant angel in the night, burned and branded now into his cerebral cortex like a third eye. But, the unrelenting programming of his sense of sight, attuned to the realities of light and shadow in the material world, persisted, and it sent a pattern into Trask's mind that suddenly leapt into meaning.

"Arnold, I think I see a boat!" Trask announced.

But Arnold was too far gone to respond. He was lost, perhaps forever, in an ocean of grief.

Through another break in the rain, Trask's initial suspicions were confirmed. *They are launching a boat*! And it appeared that the storm had begun to abate, too, at least for the moment.

Incredibly, within minutes, the rescuers were calling out, and Kerrigan's boat pulled up alongside the broken vessel.

"Hallow! Hallow!"

"We're up here!" Trask yelled out. "We're alive!" This statement of the obvious fact seemed ludicrous upon pronouncement, yet it brought joy and hope to his heart, and utter shock to the rescuers.

"Stay where you are. We'll come to you."

It was with the greatest difficulty that Trask and Arnold were helped out of their shelter in the mast, an endeavor that was, in itself, fraught with peril. But, after a time, they were both down, and back onto the half-submerged deck.

From deckside, the transformation of this once living vessel astonished Trask, but he took no time to ponder the change. They tumbled into the lifeboat that included the insistent Cassandra Wolff, and, in a few minutes, they were on shore...

Meanwhile, Eck and his men had been laying off in their wretched vessel watching quietly as the rescue transpired. No sooner had Kerrigan's boat reached shore that Eck pounced.

"They've done their work, boys. Now, we'll do ours. But, let's be quick about it, before the wreckmasters arrive."

Chapter Sixteen

The Aftermath

It is late morning now. The *Young America*, what is left of her, is perfectly visible to the assembled people on the beach. It is hard to believe how close to shore she is, 300 yards at the most. At a full moon low tide, one could probably wade out to her, and place a hand on her once proud hull. She had split in two, and the halves of her sat in the sand opposite each other like the shell of a cracked egg dropped onto a stone.

The bonfire still raged on the beach. It is raining, though of a very different sort than the night before - a steady gentle pelt of small drops that soak the already sodden earth like the small persistent tears that linger after an all-night shouting match. The wind had subsided to the rear-guard bluster of a powerful enemy that has moved on having already achieved complete victory.

Trask and Arnold are stretched out on the leeward side of one of the bonfires smothered in blankets, protected between the sail of the *Soliloquy* rigged as a windbreaker, and the hot forked spires of the bonfire. Cassandra and Dahlia are rubbing the legs, feet, arms and hands of the two men. They have been doing so for several hours now. Arnold is still crying inconsolably.

Trask has no sensation in his left foot. His boots have long since been cut off, revealing on that foot a grotesque wound. The boots were quickly grabbed by the crowd as souvenirs. Any part of the vessel, or the people who were involved in the rescue had been greedily confiscated by the crowd. Everything that came ashore is considered fair game including Trask's own chest of personal items which was broken into while he lay prone on the beach fighting for the return of sensation in his extremities.

This changed by late afternoon when Moses Howland Grinnell arrived on the beach with the wreckmasters. The wreckmasters were appointed by district to unload the cargo, tow the vessel to port and strip the stranded vessel, if necessary, to get every last penny from it. They were employed by the insurance and shipping companies in the area.

Grinnell was one of the few shipowners who supervised the salvage operations himself. For this reason, he had earned a reputation as a cold and greedy monster who held the value of material goods over that of the lives of the distressed.

He had been notified of the wreck via telegraph from the post office in Patchogue. On arrival, Grinnell checked on the status of Trask, his finest captain, and a man he held in high regard.

"Is there any hope?"

"He'll lose his leg, for sure, and, perhaps, some of his fingers," said Cassandra. "What damage there is to the nervous system, I can't yet say. He lost his son. If that's hope, then so be it."

"You there!" Grinnell suddenly shouts. "Stay away from that box, you jackal. That belongs to the Grinnell & Fish Trading Company."

The beachcomber skulked away, glancing sideways at Grinnell as he and his compatriots slithered away down the beach.

Cassandra stands up from her duties, outraged. "Mr. Grinnell, now that you've saved what little is left of your precious cargo, I will remind you, sir, that 13 people have lost their lives aboard the ship belonging to the Grinnell & Fish Trading Company."

Grinnell pauses, then turns his face slowly toward the sound of her voice. His eyes bore into hers, and, non-plussed, responds to her tirade.

"My dear sister, men have taken to the sea for centuries, and they've done so for one reason - profit. They risk their lives, and they do so willingly. I risk more money than can be earned in two lifetimes, and not just my own. Investors, people who have sacrificed *their* lives to accumulate wealth so that their children may live better than they. *That* ship, *that* cargo and, yes, *those* lives. Now, you have your job. Save whom you can, and bury the rest. I have mine. Don't get the two confused."

With that he walked away, with Cassandra starting after him. "*You're* confused. *You've* got it all backwards. It's people over profits, not the other way around. These people have lost their lives because of you. Can't you see that? Why not sell the winds of heaven that man might not breathe without a price?"

But Grinnell continued to walk stiffly down the beach, barking orders to the wreckmaster and his crew. They had already launched a boat, and were busy at work on the ship itself, picking over the vessel, stripping it even of her jibs and running gear. Much of the tea, though, was gone.

Chapter Seventeen

The Spoils

"This is a happy day," Eck said, holding a dented in cup full of whiskey aloft. "A happy, happy day."

Even Supercargo Butler was happy now, too - happy to be back in Eck's houseboat sitting around a fire; happy that the tea was finally stored away and safe; happy to be done with this ugly business that felt so much like grave robbing.

"We pulled it off, men," Eck announced. "You didn't think we could do it, but we pulled it off. More whiskey?"

Joe the Indian nodded greedily.

"No, thanks," Supercargo Butler said, "I'm just going to bed."

Eck put his arm around the burly man's shoulders. "You earned it, my friend. You earned it. The tea's safe and sound. And it's all ours, fair and square. But you're right. Rest up! You'll need your strength to start spending your share! HA! HA! HA!"

Chapter Eighteen

At Cassandra's House

Cassandra walks into the darkened room, sits on the edge of the bed, and starts dabbing Trask's head with a cold wash cloth to help bring the fever down.

"Dahlia, it's time to change the dressing, again."

Dahlia breezes into the room, concerned.

Cassandra sits the captain up, fills a drinking glass with whiskey. She holds it to his lips, "Here, drink. Drink..."

"Nooo!" he screams, resisting. In his delirious mind, crippled from pain, he figures if he doesn't drink the whiskey they won't change the dressing.

Dahlia begins to inch the bandage off his leg.

"Aaargh! Aargh!" Trask is writhing in pain.

"Drink," she insists again. This time, he does with most of it spilling out of both sides of his mouth.

The leg is gangrenous, and, for what seems to be the very first time, Dahlia sees Cassandra's face go pale from disgust. But she quickly composes herself.

"Dahlia, get me the maggots."

In what was once a kitchen pantry, now a dispensary, Dahlia reaches for a glass jar filled with a grotesque, writhing lump of white common house fly larvae, maggots. The maggots are applied directly to the infected area. Over a period of a few days, they devour their way through the infected tissue hopefully ridding the wound of the infection. It is a final strategy before resorting to amputation.

"May God be with you," Dahlia whispers, as Cassandra spoons out the maggots onto the wound.

Arnold, in the next room, is in a state of utter delirium. He continues to shiver, uncontrollably, despite the fact that he has been laid out in front of a warm fire snug with a hot water bottle, at Cassandra's half-way house for almost three days. Dahlia offers him some tea, hot gingerbread and freshly cooked chicken, but the poor man is completely unresponsive.

He refers to Dahlia as "Mama," and continues to sing the same idle sea ditty over and over again. *"They said he got his head chopped off, it spoiled his constitution..."*

There are no hospitals on Fire Island, and the nearest on Long Island is in Jamaica at least a day trip away. In this cold and with these men in this condition, it is best that they repair here at Cassandra's house of refuge located on a small sand promontory some ways down the beach.

She and Dahlia tended to beached sailors in this way. For Cassandra, it had become her work of the spirit in the world, a manifestation of her Transcendentalist beliefs. Dahlia, hired initially as domestic help when Cassandra's husband Lachlan was alive, had become her willing assistant doing "the Lawd's work." Together, they had tended to over 70 men, women and children rescued from wrecked ships on this coast.

Her home was suitable to the task, the largest abode on the island, built by Lachlan, who had inherited a fair estate from his father, a Scot. Cassandra had adapted it for its purpose over the

Cassandra's House

years, and equipped it as well as she could with medical supplies.

Cassandra was a woman of prodigious energy and keen intellect. She had been taught Latin at her father's knee, Samuel Weeks, the pastor at the Patchogue Evangelical Congregation, and was reading the classics in the ancient tongue by age seven. By the age of 16, she had been admitted at the Harvard Divinity College, one of the first women to be admitted, and surely the youngest.

Her straight line to prominence became fractured, however, during her stay at the university. In letters to her father, she began to complain bitterly about the emphasis on "dictatorial dogma" taught at the school, and lamented wistfully about her desire for a "direct experience of the divine," one that could be experienced in the "pungent tang of horse droppings, and the arrogant sway of a harlot's hips."

The young Cassandra rhapsodized about meeting a man in Concord who had lit a "divine fire in her mind," the controversial preacher, Ralph Waldo Emerson. He had established a reputation as "the people's preacher," and was building quite a following among the impressionable young people in the area.

Cassandra soon became a regular and welcome contributor at the Transcendentalist meetings at his house in Concord. His essay on "Self-Reliance" delivered at Divinity College in Harvard convinced her to drop her studies completely, and "throw herself into the arms of God."

This behavior infuriated her father who felt that his own reputation was at stake. He demanded that she return to Long Island. She refused. He withdrew her stipend. She was defiant. He cut off all contact. She happily complied.

The little girl who had been raised to think was now thinking for herself.

Her father died before a *rapprochement* could be brokered. It was only then, with him gone, that she returned to Long Island to care for her grief-stricken mother Lilian, though the townspeople never forgave her for her impudence. As the popular preacher of the Patchogue Evangelical Congregation for over 30 years, her father had a mighty and loyal following in the congregation. The funeral service was absolute torture for her. Her mother died 18-months later.

So when her husband suggested they build a house, it was Cassandra's idea to "build something by the sea." Though only across the bay from Patchogue, Fire Island represented for her the very end of the earth, a safe refuge, away from the turned heads, the averted glances, the whispers just out of earshot. She could be away from all that, and face-to-face with the water, the air, the sun, the earth and the horizon that holds them all together. A direct experience of the divine indeed, particularly during hurricane season…

Chapter Nineteen

At Grinnell's House

With his granddaughter on his knee, Moses Howland Grinnell seemed like the happiest man on earth.

"Papa...'ese," said the soft, squirming bundle of energy.

"My glasses?" Grinnell said in mock surprise. "Absolutely not."

Grinnell with his Grandchildren

" 'Ese," said the little girl. She grabbed the glasses from his face, wholly unaware of the eminent man's position in life.

"Hey!" Grinnell said, acting outraged. "Give me back my glasses!"

The little girl squealed with delight, and held the glasses behind her back.

"This one?" he asked, pointing to one of her arms. She shook her head *no*.

"This one?" he asked, pointing to the other one. She shook her head *no* again.

"It's got to be ONE of them!" he bellowed.

Then she put them on her nose, and tapped her finger on her cheek as if she were pondering something.

The small crowd assembled around the long rectangular dinner table roared with approval at this little scene, and immediately proclaimed her to be "the sweetest thing on earth." Grinnell gave her a kiss on her forehead - took back his glasses - and then showed the children his new kaleidoscope.

It had been a wonderful evening, full of lively conversation, good food and pleasant company. Two of the most prominent families in New York, the Grinnells and the Callaghans, had reaffirmed their close connection to one another.

Brandy and French Cognac in crystal snifters was served, followed by chocolate mints from Switzerland on silver trays. Grinnell then beckoned them all into the study where they were welcomed by the warmth of a well-stoked fire, and a very special guest.

"Ladies and gentlemen," Grinnell began with a flourish, "I would like to introduce you to one of the greatest entertainers of our time, a woman who has been the toast of New York, and has now returned for a limited engagement - the 'Swedish Nightingale,' Jenny Lind."

A shock of recognition passed through the crowd. Posters of her had been everywhere in recent seasons. She had radiant white skin and full red lips.

"Tonight Miss Jenny Lind will sing selections from *La Traviata*."

Grinnell began to clap, and the rest of the crowd followed suit. This truly was an unexpected pleasure.

"Thank you," she said with a curtsey. "*La Traviata* is a tale about a true and pure love between Alfredo and Violetta, a love that turns tragic through the entanglements of jealousy, misunderstanding and betrayal. The *aria* I would like to sing for you now is called "*Addio del passato*" - "Goodbye to the Past." It is sung by Violetta on her death bed. She has just been given a note by Alfredo, who has asked for her forgiveness. But, as she sings now, it is too late."

With that, the elegantly dressed star composed herself for a moment, and opened her mouth...

The sound that issued forth was supernatural in its beauty and clarity. To say it filled the room would be a gross understatement; the sound seemed unconfined by walls. It leapt out into the night, and seemed to over-arch the entire city of New York like a shimmering, crystalline gauze firmament that dripped its riches like abundant honeydew everywhere.

The small crowd in the study kept their distance, apparently fearful of being too close to the power of this voice. Each was as still as a statue, awestruck in the performer's presence. One of the ladies withdrew her kerchief, and dabbed away a sniffle and some small tears. Others soon followed. The men tried dutifully to maintain decorum, but it was unsettling to be exposed to this voice, this unmistakable manifestation of God.

The performer, for her part, seemed somehow apart from the sound that emanated from her body. She seemed moved by it, too. And yet, what strength! To channel that power with utter fidelity, and to do so gracefully. This was perhaps the most powerful thing of all...

When the *aria* was complete, there was an awkward hesitation in the crowd, still spellbound by the performance. Several of the ladies were crying openly. Grinnell lead the crowd into applause which seemed such a trifling testament to the experience of the performance. She curtseyed, maintaining protocol, and began to sing again...

When the stunning performance was over, the ladies returned to the dining room for an evening tea, and Henry Callaghan was invited to enjoy a cigar with Grinnell in a cozy ante-room at the rear of the study. This room was the inner sanctum, the seat of Grinnell's power and prestige. To be invited here was a privilege indeed, and somewhat intimidating for the uninitiated.

Grinnell decorously opened a wooden box of fresh fragrant cigars, and passed it under the noses of the men gathered together. He gestured to an elaborately carved teak matchbox on the credenza.

"One of my captains found this in Shanghai. Look at the work in the detail."

It was a rare and extraordinary object, one of the many that filled the room. This was a sanctuary of a man of means *and* taste.

The Inner Sanctum

As the men leaned back in their chairs, and enjoyed the first few aromatic puffs of perhaps the finest tobacco in the world, Grinnell raised his brandy snifter.

"To the good Congressman," he said, gesturing to Henry Callaghan, "congratulations at the onset of your fourth term in the United States Congress."

"Here, here," went the small crowd, and crystal clinked all around.

"Henry, it's such pleasure to see you and your family," Grinnell began. "What a wonderful family you have, too. You must be a proud man."

"I am, Moses," Callaghan responded, "and proud to have such a generous and hospitable friend such as you. Thank you for having us."

"It's my pleasure, Congressman," Grinnell continued. "I am, as always, at your service."

"And I, at yours," Callaghan spoke gallantly. "If there is anything I can ever do for you, Moses, please let me know."

"Henry, as you know, I have just recently suffered yet another loss at sea. The salvage operation has yet to do a full tally, but

I suspect it is close to a total loss. This is the fourth wreck off the coast of Fire Island in 18 months. At the association, my colleagues have dubbed it Wreck Valley. The better part of the trade of this entire nation comes through that route, Henry. Hundreds of thousands of shareholder dollars disappear every time one of these vessels goes down. Not to mention the loss of lives. Nine people died on the *Young America*. Nine people, nine families, just like our own.

"Fortunately, there are some stout-hearted volunteers who managed to save the life of my captain, and the cook. These people are admirable, Henry, well-intentioned. But equally so are they ill-equipped and poorly trained. There isn't much they can do. In fact, their lives are at much at risk in these operations as the people they're trying to save."

Grinnell zeroed in on his target.

"Henry, this country needs to erect and equip lifesaving station houses all along the coast staffed full-time with well-trained disciplined men to save the lives of the crew of these wrecks and, yes, as much of the goods on board as is possible. Directly, sir, I'm asking you to introduce legislation to fully fund this lifesaving service, to make it a legitimate, and perpetual service to the American people."

The directness and force of the request caught Callaghan somewhat unprepared. But he was an old hand and, like Grinnell, skilled in the art of negotiation.

"Moses, I am fully sympathetic to your plight and that of your colleagues, and I have expressed my profound sympathy at the loss of life, not only at the site of the wreck, but here in town on several occasions. It is a great and ongoing tragedy that, I agree, we must do something about. But I also must remind you, Moses, that we are a young nation with limited funds."

To let that point sink in a little, he took a puff of his cigar.

"I know it's quite dramatic, a rescue at sea. But I reckon very few of my constituents have ever seen one. I'm hard-pressed to believe there is even a mild interest for such a service among the people upon whose forbearance my office depends."

Grinnell eyed him sharply from behind a swirling veil of smoke.

"On the other hand, Moses," Callaghan continued, "as the chairman of the Appropriations Committee, I do hold considerable sway as to the future of legislation that affects the waterfront districts. Some people have even suggested that no bill can even get to the floor without going through my office first. I have bills suggested to me every day, good legislation, well-intentioned, and sometimes it gets to the point where I can't tell one from another."

He looked up at Grinnell through the gray air, to see if his message has gotten through.

"What I neyd, Moses, is a way to distinguish *this* bill from all the others, a way for it to stand out in my mind, and in the minds of my colleagues..."

Callaghan paused, then leaned forward in his chair, looking Grinnell right in the eye. The other men in the room sat mesmerized by this exchange.

"I'm sure you understand what I am saying, Moses?"

"Your point is well-taken, Henry," Moses returned, "and I'm sure you can count on the support and understanding of my colleagues at the association."

Chapter Twenty

Wild, Strong and Beautiful

Trask hears a sound like voices coming from the next room. At first he cannot distinguish them one from another. They seem to be one voice. He lets the sound waft over him like the quilt that covers his body, and seems to press him flat against the mattress. Then one voice cleaves itself from the others, a woman's voice.

It is vaguely familiar. *Cassandra.*

Trask then becomes dimly aware of a sensation, a cold wash cloth is being dabbed on his forehead. It occurs to him that Cassandra has been doing this for some time now.

Trask's attention is drawn away from her to the face of the man over the fireplace mantel. But it is difficult to focus. The image wavers, an effect of the air in front of it being heated by the three candles underneath. He looks back at Cassandra's face, which seems to be wavering as well.

"How's Arnold," Trask manages.

"He's holding his own," Cassandra lied. In fact, Cassandra believed Arnold wouldn't live through the night.

"How's my leg?" Trask ventured.

"The doctor is coming tonight. He's going to take a look at it, and let us know."

Word reached the doctor to bring his amputation tools, and Cassandra already knew what the doctor's prognosis would be.

"Josh..."

"You need to rest, Mr. Trask," Cassandra abruptly ended the conversation. "The best thing for you to do right now is rest."

"M's Wolff, the doctor is here," Dahlia announced into the room, and, on the way down the hallway away from the patient's range of hearing, she completed the announcement. "The preacher is with him, ma'am."

After greeting the two men, and the driver of their carriage, Cassandra led everyone into the room where Arnold had sung his last sea ditty. The doctor quickly pronounced Arnold dead, and Cassandra recommended to the preacher that, considering Trask's fragile physical and mental health, a quick and quiet ceremony for Arnold was called for.

The preacher stepped back from the bed, and lowered himself to one knee.

"Dear God and all your angels," he began in a whisper, "please welcome Edwin Arnold to live with you in eternity. We will all miss him here on earth, and we now humbly commend him into your loving arms. Amen."

"Amen," Cassandra replied, without taking her eyes off the image of her dead husband Lachlan propped in a picture frame on the bureau by Arnold's bed. Through tending to Arnold, she had bravely said goodbye to her husband, once again.

Her relationship with her husband had always struck her as one the strangest happenings of her life. They met, or more properly, *re*-met, at the funeral service for her father, when Cassandra caught Lachlan staring at her with unusual intensity. They both quickly looked away, it being unseemly to engage glances in that way at such an event.

Lachlan Wolff approached her after the ceremony, and offered his condolences.

"Cassandra, I knew your father well. He was a great man, a pillar of this community, and he will be sorely missed. My heart goes out to you in your grief."

He took both of Cassandra's hands, and held them outright between his own. He looked directly into her eyes; his gaze boring into her like a saber. Even for a proper ceremony such as the funeral of the local preacher, Cassandra found his manners impressive, his bearing gallant, his grooming impeccable.

In subsequent days, he came by the house to bring prepared food, and to sit with Cassandra and her mother Lilian. On one occasion, he said to Cassandra: "Miss Weeks, you probably don't remember me growing up, but I remember you. I was 16 years old, and you were six. I thought then that you were the most precocious child I had ever seen."

"Precocious?" she replied with an arched eyebrow. "Isn't that just a fancy word for fresh?"

"Hah! Some might say so. I didn't see it that way, though."

"And how *did* you see me then, Mr. Wolff?"

Wolff gathered his thoughts for a moment before settling on his answer.

"Miss Weeks, you were like a wildflower, growing wild and strong…"

"…and willful," she cut in.

Laughing. "No, I wasn't going to say that."

She examined his face closely, and then chose to move the conversation forward.

"What *were* you going to say, Mr. Wolff?"

The man's face flushed.

"I was going to say *beautiful*, Miss Weeks. Wild, strong and *beautiful*."

She lowered her eyes for a moment, then looked up again at his, not wanting to miss what might come next. This man seemed so unlikely to her. He was much too traditional, too settled.

"There are all kinds of beautiful in this world," he said softly, still looking straight at her. "But the best kind of beautiful is that which is unsullied by the traditions and conformity of Society."

Does he read Emerson? she thought.

"That which comes right from the wild is the best and most beautiful."

His eyes sparkled.

"Don't you think so?"

How had he managed this, she wondered. How had he

managed to slip right under her guard?

"Mr. Wolff, you are so kind and thoughtful for coming by as you have. My mother and I are so grateful for your kind solicitation."

"I can see I've overstayed my welcome here today."

"No, not at all."

"You're being kind. Well, goodbye then."

She looked hard after him as he walked toward the door.

"Goodbye, Mrs. Weeks," he said as he poked his head into the front room where Lilian Weeks was seated.

"I think I'm up to making a peach pie tomorrow," said Lilian. "Why don't you come by, and have some with us."

Wolff looked at Cassandra before answering, and her face did not say *no*.

"All right. I will, then. I'll come by about five o'clock?"

"Good," chirped Lilian, feeling better. "I'll make sure we have some ice cream to go with it."

"That'll be nice. I'm looking forward to it."

Cassandra bobbed up from her reverie, as the doctor took his satchel of utensils, and retreated with Cassandra, Dahlia and the preacher into Trask's room to attend to the real work of the visit, the preservation of Trask.

Chapter Twenty-One

The Ol' Stand

Joshua James passed under the sign over the front door of the tap room which read The Ol' Stand. As he walked through the front door, he was almost leveled by the smell of stale beer.

Having come from the bright sunshine, James' eyes take their time adjusting to the darkness of the space. The walls are exposed brick, poorly mortared. Bar stools are turned upside down on the tables.

Five men sit fidgety and nervous around a table in the back. From the look of them, none had ever been in a barroom during the day before. They were like choir boys in church long after the service had ended. They'd been in the space before, but for other reasons, and now seemed completely ill at ease.

After the exchange of a few uncomfortable pleasantries, James starts in.

"Gentlemen, let us call this meeting to order, the first meeting of the United States Lifesaving Service, Lone Hill Station. The first order of business is a roll call. Each man is to stand, and recite his name. Starting here with this man, and going clockwise around the table."

"Elijah Slocum..."

"Jeremiah Slocum..."

"Jimmy Gilbert..."

"Joseph Barker..."

"Abraham Century..."
"Thomas Mannering..."
"Joshua James..."

James stiffened to attention as he barked his own name. His backbone seemed like a stout pole that had been driven deep into the earth beneath his feet.

"The next order of business is uniforms," James continued. "Members of the United States Lifesaving Service are required to wear the uniform of the station at all times while on duty. Following this meeting all present are to report to Henry Jackson, the tailor, and be measured for said uniform.

"Item number three on the agenda is the matter of the station house. Samuel Thompson reports to me that the station house will be constructed and ready for occupancy on Friday, September 30. I have complete faith in this man's word and expect that it will in fact be ready on that day. Therefore, all members of this station will be reporting to the Lone Hill station house on that day at 6:00 a.m..."

The men around the table all shared the same queer fascination with Joshua James' oratory. This is not what anyone had anticipated. Lifesaving efforts had always been an entirely voluntary effort. There were loosely organized humanitarian societies dedicated to the task, and some of these men had been drawn from those ranks. When there was a wreck, word would get out, and people would do what they could.

But this, *this* felt like the army.

"Item number four on the agenda is the drill regimen. In order to have an orderly, well-run station, and so that the members of this station will be as prepared as they might be in the event of a wreck, the members of the Lone Hill station will be executing the following drill schedule..."

The men look at each other in disbelief.

James went on without pausing. "The Fire Drill will be performed once each week, sometimes at night. The Boat Drill will be performed twice each week. Signal Drill, seven times a week."

"That's once a day, Mannering," Gilbert cracked.

"The Resuscitation Drill, once a week. All men will receive additional instructions in pilot rules, lifesaving regulations and compass once a week...No drills will be held on Saturday."

"That's a relief," Gilbert jibed.

"Saturdays shall be devoted to general cleaning about the station. If the weather on any day be unsuitable for any of the prescribed drills, the keeper may substitute others on the schedule, but the required number of each kind of drill must be held."

"Any questions?"

The men were too stunned to speak.

"That being the case, the first meeting of the Lone Hill Lifesaving Service is now over. You are to re-assemble immediately outside of this building behind me as we march to Mr. Jackson's shop."

Outside, dead brown leaves littered the muddy ground everywhere. It had begun to rain again. The road was 18 inches deep of soft, runny mud.

"Companaeee! Begin with the left foot and...step, step, two, step. Step, step, two, step."

The procession trudged up the Main St. of Patchogue with James marching proudly at the head of this rag-tag band. The men huddle behind him like a pack of wild, wet and chastened hounds.

This absurd parade wound its way through town, oblivious to the curious stares of the people coming to their windows, to the giggles of the children huddled under the awnings, to the rain, the mud.

In this manner, they marched from The Ol' Stand, site of their first meeting, to the town tailor. When they arrive, they are dutifully measured for uniforms.

FIRE ISLAND

Chapter Twenty-Two

Blood Money

The moon at the end of Gracie's wharf on the East River seemed reachable. It is a swollen, bloated mass of white laboring its way up into the eastern sky. In its fullness, it draws toward it the sea which was now threatening to breach the surface of the wharf.

Eck ties off his team of two moribund horses, and stretches his arms toward the darkening sky. A slither of tobacco juice squirts out of the side of his mouth, and lands on top of a dock pile.

Waves from the bay slurp gently against the pilings underneath, like a cat licking its paws in satisfaction after a kill, and the vultures of the shoreline, the seagulls, gawking, pick at the remains of the day. The timbers of the ships tied up at dock groan like the sighs of a tired man slumping in his easy chair.

At the end of Gracie's Wharf is a lone silhouette facing out toward New York Harbor. He is as still as a dock piling, and his stovepipe hat atop his head makes him seem immense.

"Mr. Grinnell, tha' you?"

Grinnell turns toward Eck without speaking.

"Not much out there today, tide all wrong. Storm like that, sprays everything all over. Few things. Tea's all bad, couple crates. Vultures out there scooping everything up, damn their eyes."

"What have you got, Eck?"

"Sixty cases of tea, though I can't vouch for all of it. Sixteen cases rum."

"There were 500 cases of tea on that vessel!" Grinnell snaps.

"Couldn't get it all, Mr. Grinnell. Boat ain't big enough. A lot of it went bad, like I said. Fish are the happy tea drinkers now." And he laughed an odd-sounding little giggle.

"Two hundred dollars."

A look of feigned shock flits across Eck's face.

"Mr. Grinnell, as I'm sure you're aware, these are some of the finest teas in the world - you say so yourself."

"I'll pay you $200 dollars, no more,"

"Mr. Grinnell, look over yonder. See that city? There's more tea drinkers in that one city than there is sand on the beach. This tea won't be hard to get rid of, and at a price."

"Eck, this is my property to begin with."

"That's the law of the sea, Mr. Grinnell, law of the sea. Four hundred dollars ought to do it, though. What's a measly four hundred dollars to a man like you?"

"Eck, you are a thief and a coward. I'll pay you $220 for the whole batch. And if you don't take my offer, I'll come get the tea myself. There aren't many places to hide 60 cases of tea on that beach."

"You'd be surprised what you can do on that beach, Grinnell, you'd be surprised. In any case, I can see how badly you need this deal, so I'll go easy on you. I consider you a friend. I'll have the Indian bring it by tomorrow. Have my money ready."

With that, Eck tipped his hat, and walked away down the pier. Inside, he was smiling as wide as the ocean horizon. Not only had he lured the *Young America* to its demise, he stripped it of its goods, and had the pleasure of selling them back to its owner. It was a triple treat for the man who so enjoyed taking vengeance on Mankind.

Eck was from a long line of lowly slime. His father had come across from Hungary, an indentured servant, who escaped a moutain of debt, and was sold into the service of a backwoods country farmer in the Blue Ridge Mountains. For his master, he ground out a miserable subsistence until after 18 months, he couldn't take it any more, and murdered his master and wife with a hatchet, then fled north to Quebec.

There, for Eck senior, it got worse. Suffering from syphilis and a biological aversion to cold weather, he wasted away, succeeding only in impregnating a 14-year-old girl, Ida, who wandered into his ken like a lost puppy.

They made house together for awhile. He had erected a makeshift lean-to under the town dock, possibly the worst place for him in his condition. He spent his days scouring the beach for driftwood, and fishing off the pier. At night he squired his 'lovely pet,' who, it seems, was always wet, pale and pregnant. Barely able to take care of herself, she now had him, his illness and his three sons - Frank, Josh and Earl. Josh was early, and died before he was one year of age. Earl sputtered along like a wet rat without enough will to overcome the obstacles before him, wishing to crawl back into Ida, if he could, and sleep again.

Frank was the only one of the three to survive. After the rigor of childbirth and child rearing overcame young Ida, Frank Sr. brought Frank, now three-years-old, to the local convent. There the sisters raised him harshly imposing upon him the burdens that build character, the sufferings that engender sympathy with Christ on the cross.

Little Frank was up with them at 4 a.m., mass at 4:40, chores until breakfast, prayers after breakfast, chores till dinner, two hours of prayers after dinner, then, mercifully, to bed.

His father never visited him.

One person in all the world showed kindness to him - Sister Vincent. She seemed to be the youngest of the sisters in the order. She had clear translucent skin, almost blue.

One day, she took Frank aside, and crouched beside him so that her face was right in front of his. For the very first time, he saw the lines just outside her eyes. He saw the pores in her cheek, and the dryness of her lips.

"Frank, I want you to listen to me very carefully. I'm going away from here tonight. I'm going to take you with me. We're going to New York. We'll be safe. No one is going to hurt us."

FIRE ISLAND

All Frank could think of was Sister Laurentia, the Mother Superior. She had box-slapped him once, one hand placed against one cheek, and, with the other, a hand slap across the opposite cheek. She only had to do it once, and he never forgot it. It gave new meaning to the phrase "turning the other cheek."

Sneaking out the back door of the convent, his insides froze at the thought of Sister Laurentia. Surely she would come for us; she would track us down, he thought.

Sister Vincent was hardly recognizable without her tightly drawn black habit. She looked...like a woman. Frank scurried along behind her pulled by her cool hand for what seemed like forever.

When they stopped for the evening, she laid out her blanket, and hummed a sad tune. Then, she turned slightly away from him, and prayed silently over her rosary beads. They curled up together, and slept.

How strange it was to lie next to her, how frightened Frank was to do so. He could not sleep at all the first few nights, the smell of her was so pungent. She smelled like the old convent.

Once they got to New York, the nine-year-old boy was left at the New York House of Refuge, a reformatory newly opened in an abandoned federal arsenal between 22nd & 23rd Streets. Sister Vincent disappeared from his life forever.

If possible, the New York House of Refuge was more severe than anything the sisters could dish out up in Canada. The facility was run by the Reverend John Stanford, who saw to it that a "vigorous course of moral and corporal discipline" would make the 1,000 boys and girls in his care "able and obedient."

A daily journal of infractions tells all one needs to know of discipline at the New York House of Refuge.

E.D. - Paddled, with his feet tied to one side of a barrel, his hands to the other.
J.M. - Neglects her work for play in the yard, leg iron, and confined to House.
Joseph R. - Disregarded order to stop speaking, given a bit of the cat

John B. - A few strokes of the cat to help him remember that he must not speak when confined to a prison cell.
Ann M. - Refractory, does not bend to punishment, put in solitary.
William C. - Questioned guards authority, whipped.

Some street roamers responded well to this kind of approach. Others, like Eck, just got mean. And it was at the New York House of Refuge that little Frank Eck began to plot his revenge against the world.

Upon entering the Refuge, Eck was stripped and washed, had his head shaved, was given a uniform, and placed in a windowless 5 x 8 foot cell. To prevent escape, the Refuge was surrounded by a two-foot thick concrete wall. The boys spent most of their time making ladies' shoes - 60 pair a day was their quota - which were sold in the local retail shops. Eck bided his time, watching, learning, plotting, for two long-suffering years. Then, he was released to work on a whaling ship for a local captain as the ship's boy. After a horrific 18-month voyage, he took his pay, and got away with his life.

By the age of 14, he was determined to never do another honest day's work in his life.

He fell in with a group called the Daybreak Boys. No one in the gang was over 18 years old. Their specialty was to quietly row out to ships at anchor just before dawn. Once aboard, they rifled through the cargo picking the best for themselves. Then, they would quickly run their booty to the Brooklyn side where it was sold off handsomely to fences.

Daybreak Boys at Work

FIRE ISLAND

Life was good for young Eck in those days, until the local Chief of Police, George Matsell - 300 pitiful pounds of meanness and degradation - decided to rid New York of "the increasing number of vagrants, idle and vicious children who infest our public thoroughfares."

For a time, the Daybreak Boys were able to outwit this buffoon, but it was clear that the party was over. And, unless Eck wanted to go back to the Refuge, or worse, the Blackwell Island Penitentiary, he had better leave town. He sailed to Brooklyn, and kept following the shipwrecks on the beach until he reached Fire Island...

Chapter Twenty-Three

Abraham Century

"Four men to the rear to push," Joshua James intoned. "Two men to pull the mule."

The cart carrying the provisions had become stuck in a mucky morass of beach grass and thick black marsh sludge.

"Gilbert, why don't you try pushing the mule from behind. That's a good spot for you," said Elijah Slocum.

"Slocum, the only behind you should push is your ol' lady's. It's sagging something fierce."

"On the count of three: one...two...three..."

The men grunted and harumphed, but the cart was more stuck than ever, having sunk another six inches or so into the black goo. The men themselves were knee deep in the muck which made a great slooshing noise when one of them was able to extract his foot from its clutches.

"It's taken me boot! The bloody monster has eaten me boot! It's a miracle I still have me foot," shouted Skull Murphy.

Their efforts were made all the more unpleasant by the fact that horseflies, the size of large buttons, swarmed into the mix, and began nipping at exposed flesh. Gilbert, who had tied his uniform top around his waste to "get some sun," soon wished he hadn't done so.

The others suffered along with their full uniforms upon them, black wool pantaloons and petticoats, more suited for the driving gales of February than a hot August afternoon.

FIRE ISLAND

The Fire Island beach during a hot afternoon in August is an abominable prospect. There is no shade. There is no fresh water other than what you can carry with you from the mainland or preserve in rain barrels. The bleached white sand reflects the heat of the summer sun, doubling its already withering intensity. The ocean sparkles in a dazzling dance of sunny reflections paining the eye with crystalline shards of light.

The men looked like vampires caught in the sun.

It was James' idea to begin drilling prior to the completion of the station house, for "maximum preparedness." But at this point, things were not going well. Indeed, the very act of getting to the shoreline was proving to be a task that in itself was almost too great for the group to overcome.

The horse Gypsy started braying in panic. James ordered the men to unhitch her, and pull the cart out themselves.

"Rock it back and forth, men"

"Mr. Century, get with the men in the rear, and give it all you've got," James commanded.

Abraham Century

Abraham Century was 38-years-old, six feet, two inches tall, painfully quiet, stiller than a statue, and the stoutest man in the company.

When Century put his back to this task, the cart finally lurched out of the mud, and back into the sand.

Gilbert looked back at him in amazement.

Century sometimes seemed more like a tree than a man, putting roots down everywhere he stood. He was from the West Indies, though his family was originally from East Africa. The other men dreaded to be alone with him, not for any reason other than the awkward silence that surrounded him like fog.

Each of the men had, at some point, tried to make conversation with Century, but what little did emanate from his lips tended to be vague and incomplete.

"Century, how did you get involved in this unit?" one such conversation was begun by Elijah Slocum.

"Mr. James, there."

"Did he recommend you to someone?"

"I don't rightly know."

"Have you ever done this kind of thing before?"

" 'times."

Soon his partner in conversation would lose heart, and the space between them would fill up again with the vacuum of his silence. This mysterious aura, and his physical size made the man somewhat menacing. So, after a time, everyone gave up on him, and just stayed away which seemed to be the point Abraham Century was driving at all along.

The only man Century seemed to respect was Joshua James. Neither was given to speaking very much. Indeed, it seemed as though they never said two words directly to each other on any given day.

Yet, Century would do anything for the man. If Joshua James had asked him to lift that cart upon his shoulders, and carry it to the water, he would have done it, or die trying.

Some of the men resented this special relationship between James and Century. It wasn't just that he was a Negro; there was something else about Century that couldn't be ignored - he couldn't swim.

FIRE ISLAND

Chapter Twenty-Four

The Red Book

"What are you doing?" Trask snapped angrily.
"Cold compress. Keeps your fever down."
"What time is it?"
"11:30."
"Here, drink this. It's hot lemon tea."
"What, no more whiskey?"
"You're not out of the woods yet. Drink it all, as hot as you can take it. Then go back to sleep."
"Yes, ma'am," he said with a sarcastic gloss.

As he sipped his tea, he watched Cassandra's hands as she was folding laundry. Trask was fascinated by their crisp and quick movements, the veins budding with life, the nimble manner in which her fingers moved. They seemed so in touch with the real objects of the world. It seemed as if there were no barriers whatsoever between her mind and heart, her hands, and those things that make up the world. There was a direct connection - without guile, without self-consciousness.

She sat on the edge of the bed, and propped her leaning body up with an arm behind his back. It was only for a few moments, but Trask could feel an electric charge, like his hormones were iron filings, and she was a magnet scrambling them into a new pattern.

"Mr. Trask, I found this among your things." It was Josh's red logbook! "I kept it aside, and dried it out for you, when you're ready to look at it."

Cassandra knew what this book meant. In fact, she had read every word as she carefully separated and dried each individual page. The duty had become a sort of prayer vigil during the long days and nights of Trask's delirium. When the pages were dry, Trask's fever would end.

Trask looked at it, and sucked in a little gasping gulp of air. He hadn't thought about the logbook since he had found it in Josh's cabin.

"Put it over there for now," he said gesturing to the table. "I don't think I can read anything right now."

"Would you like me to read it to you?" she asked.

"No," Trask replied, "I'll read it on my own, when I'm up to it. Thank you."

Cassandra complied. The placement of the red book on the night table immediately tilted the balance of the entire room; it became the new fulcrum for Trask's entire universe.

The instant she walked out of the room, Trask could not resist the pull of its gravity. He reached for it, and held it in both hands, unopened, in front of his face. Trask pulled open the front cover, and peeked at the first facing page. The rescue ordeal had blurred the black ink of the careful script thereon, but it was still legible. In his son's handwriting, it read, "The Log of the *Young America*, by Mate Joshua Trask."

The book suddenly felt as heavy as a stone tablet, and the wavering of the air began again. Trask lowered it to his lap where he was quickly reminded that one of his legs was missing. For a time, he watched the fire's shadows yawning across the ceiling; then he slipped off to sleep.

After a time, Cassandra returned to the room to stoke the fire. She saw the red book, smiled, and put it back on the night table. She looked hard at Trask's face, and saw the pain etched there, even in repose. She pulled the quilt over the length of his body, and tucked it in gently under his sides. With her arms straddling his frame, her body hovered for a moment over his prone figure. This close, all the quirky flaws in his face were apparent. She noticed the nubbly little mounds of hair that made up his beard, the dried flakes of skin that covered his lower lip. She could smell him, the essence of who he was, woven closely around his body. It was his smell - crackling, brisk, outdoors - that made her insides freeze. She remembered Lachlan for a moment, and one time in particular when they had been so physical together. Her body shuddered, and the skin on her back tingled up her spine.

How she missed that now. *Right now...*

Cassandra caught herself, and shame seized her. She withdrew from the bed, from the closeness to Trask, and cursed herself silently for her soft-heartedness.

It had been six years, she thought, time enough to grieve? But what of her work? She had committed herself to it. And Trask? What did she know of him, really?

She tossed a couple new logs on the fire, tended it with the poker, and watched as it blazed anew. Her eyes drifted up with the flickering shadows, and alighted again on her husband's face.

Lachlan had died in the explosion and subsequent fire of the steamboat *Henry Clay* in the Hudson River on July 28, 1852. In a foolish display of bravado, the captain of the *Henry Clay* had engaged a rival steamer, the *Armenia*, in a race down the river. After several hours of full-out speed, the overworked boilers of the *Henry Clay* exploded, and fire engulfed the vessel.

Lachlan had survived the explosion and fire, but drowned while attempting to help other victims of the disaster. His body was never recovered.

Even now she still felt pain, not from pity for herself, and certainly not pity for Lachlan - he was in a better place, and in no pain, she was convinced - no, what hurt her still was that she could never make anything up to him again. She could never undo any hurt she may have caused him, could never retract any words mis-spoken, could never treasure any moments with him for so many that had been thoughtlessly mis-spent. It was irrevocable. He was gone. And she still had trouble reconciling herself to that.

She exited the room without looking back at Trask...

FIRE ISLAND

Chapter Twenty-Five

The Party

"Up y'r bun, mate! *Eeyack*! Up y'r bun!" said the bossy parrot as Frank Eck entered The Ol' Stand.

A black piano player swayed rhythmically behind the keys, his eyes half-closed, enraptured with the sound that seemed to emanate from his own fingers. Michael, the venerable bartender, tended to each of his charges at the bar with solicitude and discretion. The waiter girls tirelessly worked the room, keeping everyone's glass full. A dance and comedy troupe called the *Saratoga Swingers* were due on stage any minute. Spirits were high on this Saturday night, perhaps, a bit too high.

Eck, Joe the Indian and Supercargo Butler found an open table in the back. Three ladies of uncertain reputation soon joined them.

"This is the fruit of our labors, men." It was so loud in the bar that Eck was nearly shouting across the table to be heard.

"It's just like I said, Butler. I told you we would live like kings. Look at these lovely ladies. Holding onto our arms, and laughing at our jokes."

The fattest of the three girls looked at the others and giggled.

"It's all come true, hasn't it boys?"

Eck nodded his head at a passing waitress who promptly served them with fresh drinks all around.

"To my lovelies!" he toasted with grandeur. The lewd lumps of color and cloth raised their glasses, too, as coyly as they could manage.

"Grinnell is a fool," Eck said a little less audibly as he leaned conspiratorially across the table. "I've got more of his tea now than he does, plus we're living high off his money. We're not going to dump all this tea on the market now. We're going to *ease* it out. We're going to live on it a good long time. I've got people banging down my door for that tea. People are crazy for the stuff in New York. It's as good as gold, men, as good as gold."

The ladies continued to sip from their drinks, though their eyes were furtively scanning the room.

"And this is just the beginning, men," Eck said with a flourish, "*just* the beginning. Do you realize the treasures that are on those vessels - gold, spices, rum, peanuts, cotton, whatever you can think of is going right past our nose. And it's ours for the taking. Easy pickings, right off our shores. When a ship goes aground, that's it, up for grabs."

Supercargo Butler and Joe the Indian dully followed Eck's reasoning as best they could. The ladies had become distracted by the dashing gentleman on stage, the Master of Ceremonies for the *Saratoga Swingers*.

"We'll be buying out people like Grinnell in no time," said Eck, carried away with his own hyperbole. "They'll be reserving a table for us at the Merchant's Association, and naming buildings and streets after us. Why not? This is America, isn't it, land of the free. Well, we're Americans! And this stuff is free. Ha-ha!"

"Who are you kidding," Butler replied bitterly. "I'm not American, and neither is Joe here. And where are *you* from? Quebec? Where the hell is that? You're no more American than me and Joe."

"Butler, that's my point exactly," Eck replied nimbly. "This *whole country* is up for grabs. *Nobody* is from here. It's like the great land grab out west. The first one there wins. *Everyone* is out for themselves. You're waiting for some Big Daddy out there to give it to you. Meanwhile, while you're waiting, they keep taking it from you. Don't you see that? *Nobody* is going to *give* it to you here. You've got to take it, before they take it from you."

It was the same tireless Eck logic, forcefully applied, that was just enough to overcome the resistance of a whiskey-fogged brain.

"Butler, I don't know how I can make it clearer to you," Eck went on. "Here we are, finally getting the first small taste of the good life, and you're ready to abandon ship."

"Abandon ship?" Butler feebly replied.

"It sounds that way, Butler. It sounds that way," Eck said regretfully as he returned to his drink.

The music from the honky-tonk orchestra fired up at that moment, drowning out all hope of a cross-table conversation. As the dancing girls hit the stage, the crowd began to whoop and holler.

Eck leaned over to the girl next to him, and slipped her a single one-dollar gold coin. He whispered in her ear, "Chloe, now be a good girl and help Butler understand what some of the finer things in life are all about tonight..."

FIRE ISLAND

Chapter Twenty-Six

By the Light of Her Eyes

Through the doorway to the hall, Trask, from his half-open eyes, sees Cassandra Wolff fixing herself in the hallway mirror. She rigorously pulls her hair back from her face, and ties it with a fastidious bolt of scotch plaid fabric, her hands confidently working as if they each had brains themselves.

With the quick task complete, she turns her head slightly to see how it looks, tilts her chin downward a touch, and gives the hair bow a little fluff with her hand.

With that, she breezes down the hallway and into his room.

"How are you this evening, Mr. Trask?"

"Missing a leg, but thank you for asking," Trask says dryly.

With that, she busies herself about some housecleaning tasks in the room.

Trask notices the hair bow again. How quickly she had tied it, and yet how elegant it seems. Her brown hair flecked with red highlights, tightly constrained by the fabric, seemed regal, like a thoroughbred in light harness prancing around the paddock with its head cocked in the air.

"It's time to exercise your leg," she said suddenly. "Sit up on the side of the bed."

"How is it?"

"I'll let you keep that one," she said, "*if* you do your exercises like I tell you."

Cassandra sits on the bed next to him, closer, he thought

for a moment, than was called for. Being within two feet of her was to enter an electric field supercharged with possibility. This close, actually touching, and his neurons were overloaded with stimulus.

Trask shakes off this momentary distraction, and concentrates on the task at hand, the slow methodical lifting of his right leg, first at the ankle, then at the knee, then at the hip. For the first few repetitions, she assists him, easing the burden of the weight of his own body.

Then Dahlia enters the room with a question. Cassandra raises herself up, and turns around to answer. But as she does, her body lingers back, her hip gently grazing his shoulder, loitering there, in contact. It distracts Trask for those few moments; to draw back away from this would seem to be an affront, like harshly declining an invitation. She was apparently unaware of what she was doing at all.

When this brief encounter with Dahlia ends, Cassandra directs Trask to continue his repetitions until he has completed 10. Then she goes back to her housekeeping. At one point, as she dusts the objects in the room, she picks up the red book on the nightstand.

"I found this on the bed last night," she says. "Did you read it?"

"No," he says through clenched teeth as he raises his leg, "I still can't focus." He drops his leg, and forcefully exhales. "That's it, I'm done. That's 10."

"It was 12, actually."

Trask flops back on the bed. "But who's counting," he says between air gasps.

Cassandra leaves the room, her chores done, and comes back with a silver pot of tea on a rolling tray.

"How do you like it?"

"Real tea? Sugar, too! One lump, thank you."

"As you wish," she says, gently mimicking the manners of a domestic maid.

She helps Trask prop himself with pillows, and serves his cup with an air of propriety. The taste of the tea was deep and satisfying. It instantly makes Trask feel stronger than he could remember. Cassandra pulls the rocking chair a little closer to the nightstand, and then serves herself.

After several silent sips, she opens the red logbook, and begins to read by the light of the candles on the nightstand. Trask does not try to stop her...

April 13, 1857: *Today, a great omen, that augers well for our voyage. A large eagle, after sailing in the air of this busy city, so unlike its usual haunts, perched upon the truck of the foremast of the Young America. He sat there for some time, looking down in solemn dignity upon the busy scenes beneath him. He rested awhile, until his presence attracted a large number of spectators, then spread his wings, and took to flight again, lingering for a few gyrations, over South Street, then soaring off into a proud future.*

Cassandra pauses, and sips her tea.

"I remember that eagle," Trask says. "It was one of the strangest things I've ever seen. Nobody in living memory had seen a bald eagle in Manhattan. At the time, I thought it was a good omen as well..."

Cassandra continues.

April 15, 1857: *Today we embark on our great journey. It has taken us weeks to prepare, and load the vessel. And now she is full to the gunwales. Everything finally seems to be in order, (that is, to the captain's satisfaction, of course.) It's a wonder she can still float! But now, there is nothing to do, but shove off, across the open ocean, and onto China! Father is quite anxious, ill-tempered and cross. I'm told that he settles in after being at sea awhile. Let's hope. Otherwise, it will be a long trip for us all.*

Joshua and his Logbook

"Reads more like a diary than a mate's log," Trask grumbles.

Cassandra ignores his comment, and continues:

April 16, 1857: *The winds are fair, the seas are calm, and we have the seagulls to see us off. A heady start to our journey, indeed! I am so happy to be underway, my heart could burst. We all busied ourselves about the ship in a frenetic pace. Some of the cotton shifted down below, but no damage. It was quickly put right. Steady ahead!*

How odd it seemed to Trask to be laying in this strange bed, missing a leg, and listening to this woman he hardly knew read to him the intimate jottings of his lost son. But as he listened, all the memories of that voyage east came alive for him again.

How well it had begun! What fair winds they had across the Atlantic! But, all along, he was haunted by something an old captain once told him at Brown's shipyard when he was an apprentice, and his head was as soft as the inside of a melon.

"There's a certain amount of ill fortune on every voyage, William. Beware those voyages that begin well. There's sure trouble coming."

Chapter Twenty-Seven

The Service

The *Audacious* was a proud piece of equipment, and Joshua James and his crew could hardly believe their good fortune when it was delivered, on schedule, to the site of their soon-to-be-built station. It lifted everyone's spirits just to see her, and the men seemed to walk a little taller just having the *Audacious* on hand.

Built at the shipyard of William Henry Webb in New York, *Audacious* was 23 feet long and six feet wide. It had a round bilge, sloping transom, and a slightly rockered plank heel. It was a yawl, a double-ender, with the stem and stern alike, constructed of white cedar planks over sawn frames fastened by neat copper rivets.

Audacious was light enough to be transported by cart over soft beach sand, and its lithe construction enabled it to be launched directly into the surf. Yet it was strong enough to stand up to brute battering of the waves.

It was James' idea to perform the initial boat launching drill at night, in bad weather, to simulate the actual conditions likely to be encountered during a real rescue. Thus far, the drill was not going well.

For the third time, *Audacious* had capsized, and the men had to set her aright with great difficulty.

"Mr. James, sir, give it a rest, will ya'?" said Jimmy Gilbert on behalf of the other men. "The men here are freezing. Face it, the surf's just not right for launching tonight."

James, bailing with the other men, was breathing deeply, the harsh tang of the briny air banging at the limits of his lungs. He stared deep into Gilbert with a quizzical look on his face.

"This surf should be child's play, Mr. Gilbert," he said. "What if there's a wreck on the bar tonight. We'd have no choice, but to launch in any surf."

"But there *is* no wreck tonight, Mr. James. You know it, I know it, and I'll be damned if the boat doesn't know it, too. *It* doesn't want to go in that water either!"

The men laughed all around - except Abraham Century who glowered off to one side.

James drew himself up to his full height, which was less than six feet, and stood ramrod straight. "I suppose you're right, Mr. Gilbert. The men *are* tired and wet and cold. And the surf *is* nasty. Yet, I remind myself at times like these of the people who perished on board the *Young America*, the *Louis V. Place*, the *Prince Natchez*, and hundreds of other ships on this coast. Most died within sight of land, the only thing standing between them and salvation was a good boat, and some hardy men to launch it."

James' crusty formality was evident even here in the depths of the darkness on the unadorned surfline. He was obviously unaware of the gobs of sea-goo hanging off his beard. Wholly un-self-conscious, he continued, absorbed in the allegiance to a vision only he could see.

"Mr. Gilbert, I am constrained by my conscience as well as the conditions that challenge us. And, if the men are up to it, I'm for giving it one last attempt here today, one last shot at ending this bleak night on a high note."

He looked around at the men, now spellbound by the peroration coming from this quixotic figure. "That is, if the men are up to it."

There was no one, not even Gilbert, who could resist that challenge.

"Alright," Gilbert begrudgingly assented, voicing the will of the crew. "One last time."

"Then get her in position, men." James announced. "Nose into the netherlands! This time we'll get it right. On the slatch tide. Wait for my command."

James watched the surf carefully as the men spun *Audacious* around on her transom. The rule of thumb was that at every seventh wave you could count on a slackening of the surf, the *slatch* tide. James counted through a couple cycles, then saw his opportunity.

"Now, men. Shove 'er in!" James commanded. At his signal, the men pushed together entering into the frosty surf up to their waist yet again. They scrambled aboard over the gunwales into position at the oars with James, the last aboard, catapulting over the stern.

Audacious was afloat!

James manned the long sweep oar which steered the vessel from behind. He stared out over the bow of the vessel into the breakers. The men manned three pairs of parallel oars to the side, double banked on three narrow thwarts. They looked directly at James, and tried to follow his every direction.

"Port oars, pull! Starboard, ease...Together now, stroke. Stroke. Stroke."

Again and again the boat was flooded, and driven astern by

the waves, but the buoyancy of the craft allowed it to remain afloat. It maneuvered well in tough surf.

"Row now, men," James commanded. "Row for all you're worth."

Row the men did, stroke after stroke, the breakers pounding the small boat, and sending sheets of spray up over the game vessel. James held onto the sweep oar, occasionally leaning on it with his chest to force it laterally through the water. At other times, the oars would lift clear out of the surf, offering no resistance to the men whatsoever. James was determined to get clear of the surf zone.

Once *Audacious* plowed its way past the breakers, James was clearly elated. Even in the darkness, his eyes were dancing sparks of light, and he started humming a tune to himself. The men stroked on, in rhythm, and the prow of the *Audacious* knifed its way happily through the yielding water.

Time seemed to disappear; the distance between the men seemed to evaporate. They were one, a unit. And for one happy half-hour they remained that way, traversing parallel to the shoreline, making good headway, working the boat to their will. James commands were followed directly, without interference. The sea, suddenly, was an ally.

"I think that's enough," James finally said. And, with that, the crew pointed *Audacious* back to shore. With muscles happily tired, they laid her up.

Chapter Twenty-Eight

There The Dragons Be

August 23, 1857: *This day we finally sailed into Canton Harbor. We approached through Whampoa, Canton's seaport, about 14 miles away, and have been escorted by pilot craft the entire way. The vessels at sail here are strange, and majestic sights. They are everywhere with their brightly colored sails, and their strange upturned transoms. All the talk of pirates has proved untrue. Indeed, we were given quite a welcome on our arrival. Everyone waved, and flags of welcome were run up every mainmast. The air is fragrant with the smell of spices and tea. The crew is overjoyed. Land at last!*

August 24, 1857: *The pilot craft escorted us to a dock just off an impressive row of houses, called factories, where the goods would be stored. We soon learned that we were confined on board, or to these factories to offload goods. The crew's euphoria upon reaching land has quickly dissipated, and the talk has turned to suspicion of our 'yellow hosts.' Our first guest on board was Hoppo, the linguist. He is a small man who has quickly proven himself to be an unscrupulous rogue. He continually assures us that he is working in our favor, despite the overwhelming evidence to the contrary. He cannot be trusted, yet what are we to do? He is the designated runner between The Young America and the Hong merchants, and seems to be the only person in all of Canton who can speak and understand English. He does quite evidently understand how to count money, because granting him steady consideration seems to suddenly improve our position with the merchants.*

August 27, 1857: *Father is complaining about the imperial duties to be paid on our goods. It seems as though the Chinese view us as "barbarians bringing tribute to the Celestial Empire," and not as equal trading partners.*

There are port charges, charges for inward and outward pilotage, linguist and comprador's fees, imperial duties and more amounting to a total of $1,100. Fortunately for us, unlike European vessels, these duties do not have to be paid in gold or silver, but can be exchanged for goods.

We did, however, receive a fair price for our Ginseng, getting $180 a picul. The Chinese hold the herb in very high regard - it is used as a medicinal cure-all - and ours had survived the voyage very well.

The consignee secured the ship, and received the cargo into the warehouse. Our duties were accounted for to the penny. Houqua, the Hong merchant with whom we were trading, was accurate, punctual, intelligent and a man of great honor. On one occasion, he discovered an accounting error in his favor. This imbalance was immediately corrected with humble apologies, and an offer of tea in his room. This was apparently a high honor, an invitation not normally extended, and my father and I accepted immediately, not wanting to offend the man.

Houqua, the Hong Merchant

"Houqua!" Trask suddenly blurts out from his position on the bed. "Perhaps you were right, my friend. We *are* barbarians, we Americans." He takes another sip of his brandy. "And now, I'm a one-legged barbarian! Without a ship! Hah!"

The bitterness of his misfortune oozed out of every pore. Cassandra, sensing that it was unwise to continue, closed the book, and placed it on the nightstand.

"Mr. Trask, why don't you get some sleep," Cassandra offered.

"Why don't you just leave me alone," he snapped with sudden vehemence. "LEAVE ME ALONE!!! GET OUT OF THIS ROOM

RIGHT NOW, AND LEAVE...ME...ALONE!!!"

Cassandra is stunned and hurt by this ugly outburst, but she continues to look straight at his eyes for several moments. There, she sees dragons. Yellow and orange spikes of flame heaved from their flaring nostrils, scales like green steel refracting dull light like blunt knives, eyes as hard as red sapphires

When she could no longer stand the look of it, her eyes fill with tears, and her chin begins to quiver. She flees the room, and slams the door behind her.

Trask raises himself from the bed, and grabs his crude crutch. He paces the room - first the crutch, then his foot, then the crutch, then his foot. For three hours, he hobbles this way. On the nightstand is an opened letter from Grinnell inviting Trask to dinner in Manhattan, two days hence. If nothing else, Trask is determined to walk into that restaurant, unaided, with his head held high.

FIRE ISLAND

JOHN J. STEVENS

Chapter Twenty-Nine

When Half-Gods Go

Give All to Love

GIVE all to love;
Obey thy heart;
Friends, kindred, days,
Estate, good fame,
Plans, credit, and the Muse—
Nothing refuse.

'Tis a brave master;
Let it have scope:
Follow it utterly,
Hope beyond hope:
High and more high
It dives into noon,
With wing unspent,
Untold intent;
But it is a god,
Knows its own path,
And the outlets of the sky.

It was never for the mean;
It requireth courage stout,
Souls above doubt,

Valour unbending:
Such 'twill reward;—
They shall return
More than they were,
And ever ascending.

Leave all for love;
Yet, hear me, yet,
One word more thy heart behoved,
One pulse more of firm endeavour—
Keep thee to-day,
To-morrow, for ever,
Free as an Arab
Of thy beloved.

Cling with life to the maid;
But when the surprise,
First vague shadow of surmise,
Flits across her bosom young,
Of a joy apart from thee,
Free be she, fancy-free;
Nor thou detain her vesture's hem,
Nor the palest rose she flung
From her summer diadem.

Though thou loved her as thyself,
As a self of purer clay;
Though her parting dims the day,
Stealing grace from all alive;
Heartily know,
When half-gods go
The gods arrive.

That was it, Cassandra thought upon reflecting on the poem, a radical freedom – to follow love, to follow it *utterly* – to *give all* for it.

Love *requireth courage stout, Souls above doubt, Valour unbending.*

Surely here Emerson is writing not just about physical love – *Eros* – but also about a higher love, a purer love, a Divine Love – what Christians call *agape* – a love like that God has for everyone and everything, regardless of circumstances, regardless of feelings, of passion.

How often do we shun God, ignore Him, or directly insult Him – still, he continues to shine His love to us – like a star to the earth. This is *agape*.

And yet, Emerson counsels that we

> *Keep thee to-day,*
> *To-morrow, for ever,*
> *Free as an Arab*
> *Of thy beloved.*

Cassandra reads those lines again and again. "*Keep…Free as an Arab of thy beloved.*"

And, at the end,

> *Though thou loved her as thyself,*
> *As a self of purer clay;*
> *Though her parting dims the day,*
> *Stealing grace from all alive;*
> *Heartily know,*
> *When half-gods go*
> *The gods arrive.*

When half-gods go, the gods arrive…

Cassandra turned that phrase over in her mind. Again, Emerson seemed to be communicating directly to her.

Half-gods – that was Trask - when they go, the gods arrive.

Trask is gone, the gods will arrive, she thought, and a feeling of certainty settled into her soul.

It's true, that *was* the way of her life. She *had* always oscillated between the things of this world, and the things of heaven.

Cassandra was perpetually torn between these two worlds, not quite serving two masters, as Jesus warns against in the Gospel, but serving one with complete intensity, with a vivid fervor, then, just as suddenly, serving the other with equal intensity. Not two, *one* - then the other.

Trask had become a focus of her life – despite her best efforts against this. She had always been careful to keep personal feelings for those she cared for cordoned off somewhere in her heart. It hadn't been hard. She was not attracted to any of the men she had nursed back to health.

But Trask was different. Perhaps it was that he had just lost a son, and so she pitied him; perhaps it was that he was unmarried, and so he was available to her; perhaps it was that he was handsome, and so she desired him.

Or perhaps not – these things seemed so plain, so mundane. Perhaps her attraction was simply the yearning of elements to join together – the way hydrogen is attracted to oxygen, how it wants to attach itself to it, hungers for that connection, and is forever restless without it. Traveling the unknown universe forever, pining for some sort of elemental bonding, the hydrogen atom knows only loneliness, knows only this, and does not know what it does not know. Does not know what it would be like, what it would *feel* like, to make that magic connection, that glorious collaboration, that attachment to that which is not itself, which is completely other than which it itself knows.

And from this – *water*!

What does a single hydrogen atom know of water?! What could it know of this in advance?

You can *think* that you might feel something like happiness at some point in the future, but, until you actually *feel* happiness, you cannot *know* happiness. And you cannot *think* your way into feeling something, or *will* your way into feeling something.

But what the hydrogen atom knows, and what Cassandra knows, is a vague gnawing restlessness, which does not feel like a vague gnawing restlessness; it doesn't feel like anything at all. It is simply the medium in which she moves, surrounding her, like air to a tree, water to a fish. It is in the atom as it is in Cassandra, part of the air when she takes a breath, part of the water when she takes a drink.

A fish cannot *feel* that it is in water. The fish is wet, but all it knows is wet, so therefore it does not know wet, because it does not know dry.

And Cassandra does not know loneliness, nor this restless craving, but the Force of Attraction is strong, unrelenting, and it works on the human heart as it works on the earth and the moon. As she gets close to Trask, she feels his pull. It was a physical thing, a real thing that manifested itself between them. She was sure he felt it, too, though she was loath to acknowledge it. It worked on her day after day, shift after shift. At first she didn't recognize it as such; she thought she was sick; she thought it was her time too soon. She asked Dahlia to feel her brow.

"T'ain't fever you've got, ma'am," Dahlia said with a wry smile.

But now he was leaving. She knew why. Grinnell would offer him a job, and Trask would not be able to turn him down.

She felt a pang now that she couldn't shake – after one day, it was there; after two days, three days – there. A persistent pain, like a splinter in her heart.

When half-gods go, the gods arrive…

God would now return to her from the other side of the world, still shining, never-changing, steadfast, unalterable. He would welcome her back into His warmth – shining – and they would embrace each other again. There would be no recriminations – no regrets, no backward glances. She would bloom within his constancy. No love on earth could satisfy her like this Love.

When she and Lochlan met, all of her studies, her divine yearnings, seemed to evaporate like a pool of water on a hot day. He became that intense point of her passion, and she poured herself into it – into him – with everything she had.

He became for her a portal through to a great undiscovered universe; a world of smell and light and sound, a world of touch in which his fingers simply traveling across the muscular ridge of her spine could inspire alarms of delight in her.

He was the nail; she the hammer – and she focused every bit of her strength and focus into the head of that nail, and drove it, blow after blow, deeper into her heart. She felt the pang of love, as she drove this nail of hers.

Clank!
Deeper.
Brang!
Oh!
Clink!
(Again!)
Brank!
Ooh...

With each splash of purple blood, God's face blanched a bit – the color drained – till He faded into nothingness before the natural world.

Oh, He was still with her, like night waiting on the other side of the earth, but, with Lochlan, it was time to play in the daylight, in the warmth.

God smiled, and said to her –

"Play, *my child. Enjoy my paradise. I have made it just for you. Feel that sun? Smell the fragrant air? Your skin – have I not made it quick to respond to the touch? Look at your hair – see how the sun dances, and skips upon it? Your lips are heaven on earth, each nerve eager for a man's touch. This man I have sent you – his lips are parched and cracked, waiting for the moisture yours will bring. His brow is crinkled with care; he knows not which way to go. You will become his light, and he yours, for you will see in each other joy, power, laughter, love and tenderness."*

In times like this, it occurred to her that the real world, was perhaps not *either / or* – *either* the world of the spirit *or* the world of the flesh – the real world felt to her like an bolt of sunlight that oscillated between these two apparently contradictory poles. The nature of this real world was not fixed as either high or low, dark or light, spirit or flesh. It was high *then* low; dark for a long time, *then* suddenly light. Spirit, intensely; then flesh, intensely.

With Lochlan she shot through the meridian between spirit and flesh like a cannonball - smashing all the markers of her normal orientation in the doing.

Now on the other side of this line, people wondered…

Hanging onto his arm as she walked him through town?

But Cassandra and Lochlan were oblivious – they seemed to be floating over the ground in a pink bubble together – a pink bubble that protected them completely from the normal slights and sharp elbows of life with other people.

In this way they traveled together, past what now seemed like a fantastic parade of far-off sounds, and forms with soft blurry edges. Their world had changed! Now everything was seen anew – not through one's eyes alone, but also through those of another.

And in this dream, they passed unto the altar. It mattered not to her where they were to be married – the politics of this choice seemed so trivial now. As a younger girl, she thought that she might like to be married on the beach – in the open air – under the sunny smile of God's blue sky. But like her nearness to God, the distance between her and her old ideas was fading to some faraway place, too. What mattered was that she and Lochlan were to be together. Whether it was to be in a church, in a house, or on a ship – it really didn't matter.

The notion of ETERNITY entered her mind, too. I will be with him for all of this life, she thought, and for all the *next* life, too! We will be together FOREVER !!!

This thrilled her and, for the first time in her life, she was not afraid of ETERNITY, which until that point, had been perhaps the most harrowing thought of all.

ETERNITY? No time? A place without time? Can there BE a place without time? No!! Then what is it? Without an end, would you not be stuck there? *Forever?* With no end, and no possibility of ever escaping?

It had seemed to her to be the very definition of Hell.

But to be with Lochlan there – wherever, whatever *there* was or is - seemed more than comforting. In fact, there was a certainty about the thought that was undeniable to Cassandra. She was sure she and Lochlan were to be together forever, surer of this than of anything in her life.

And with this certainty there came a peace, an overwhelming feeling that suffused her entire being - body and soul and mind. ETERNITY now seemed to her to be the most beautiful thing there could be – she felt the PEACE of it – she caught a glimpse of what it could be, of what it is.

Where to get married?

How could this little issue here on Earth cause even a tiny ripple in the fabric of this everlasting continuum of Peace, Love and Joy.

She was still sure she would spend Eternity with Lochlan, but here she was on Earth – six years to the day since she'd been held by him for real – in the flesh…

Chapter Thirty

On the Street of Ships

"Let's take a cigar walk, William," Grinnell offered to Trask. It had been a charming evening between the two men at The Porter House on John Street, one of the finest German establishments in Manhattan.

The Porter House was neat and attractive with polished counters, brass railings burnished like gold, and a huge looking-glass reflecting back the elegant decanters and bottles in the rear-rack of the mahogany bar. Trask didn't want to leave, but the opportunity of a cigar in the open air with his old boss was too appealing.

"William," Grinnell started, addressing the subject of the wreck for the first time, "I've been quite worried about you. Inquired about you every day while you were under care. I can't tell you how pleased I am to see you up and around."

"Short a leg, of course," Trask responded.

"Knowing you, William, I'm confident that this small detail will not get in your way." With that, Trask accepted Grinnell's light of his cigar, and took several quick and shallow draughts from the freshly burning tobacco.

They turned their way north up South Street passing Burling Slip, a busy place, even now, as it approached evening. The slip was thick with river craft and coasting vessels tied up so close that they appeared to be a floating city. Tropical fruits were in from the West Indies. These had to be delivered to the market before daylight the following morning, and the men were working at top speed unloading baskets and barrels. The pier itself was crowded with carts drawn by careworn horses with their heads down, familiar with the uneven planking of the piers, their masters urging them through this unnatural jungle.

"I've been to Rome, William," Grinnell mused. "It's built for beauty. I've been to Paris; built for love. But New York...*New York* was built for business. The commerce of the nation, right here, the lifeblood of the empire! Even at night, bustling with business."

"It is quite a sight," Trask responded, "but I feel like a stranger now. Like a stranger in a land I once knew."

"Oh, you'll get over that. It's been a few months cooped up in a house. Give yourself a chance. Breathe the air. Look at the men. Look at the men on that ship!"

Grinnell pointed to Peck Slip where the coasters were in with their catch of the day. There they saw a brawny set of men with bare legs and arms gathered over their burgeoning haul, glistening in the pale light. The sails clung loosely about the masts dripping with spray. Lanterns hung about the vessel, or carried on board, spread an odd illumination as they swayed to and fro'. The moon refracted on the East River behind them.

The Johnnies, the 'lumpers...

"Those are *your* kind of men, Trask," Grinnell continued. "The Johnnies. The 'lumpers. Old Jack! These are men fit for adventure. And they need a strong hand, William. A *strong* hand."

Grinnell let that thought hang in the air as the accordion music from the sailor's boarding houses on Cherry Street filled the space between them. They walked on a little further being jostled by a steady stream of men - longshoremen, sailors, stevedores, shop clerks, loungers, wharf rats, the ragged and the rugged, the prosperous and those striving to supplant them. Occasionally, one or another would recognize Grinnell, and tip his cap.

Then they came upon a hundred or more longshoremen standing in two long lines facing each other at the Pine Street pier. The men were competing for drinks playing a game of "hop-skip-and-jump" while they waited for their next assignment.

Presently a dark man stepped in front of this ragged crowd. He was the boss stevedore seeking a few hands to help unload one of the Black Ball packets. The men chewed their quids in expectation, eyeing this grave man with respect and suspicion. Slowly, he paced up and down the line, and finally nodded to one of the men, who left the ranks, and walked toward the ship.

Again and again he paced out his steps, holding this unruly crowd in his thrall, saying nothing more than "You, there!" until about a dozen men had been selected.

"There's a rough justice to it all," Grinnell spoke. "I've seen it time and time again. The strong survive."

Walking on a little further they came upon the dry docks at Noah Brown's shipyard.

"Remember this yard, William?"

"How could I forget? I left one of my best fingers there."

"It's still the best shipyard here in New York. I've commissioned another vessel from them, 750 tons. And there it is, through the fence you can see her ribbing."

It was dark, but nevertheless the ebony bones of this mammoth were evident in silhouette against the starlit sky.

"750 tons!" Trask wondered. "Look at the bow! How is she going to sail?"

"Some of my colleagues don't believe she *will* sail, past Sandy Hook anyway. Griffith told me the bow was built at the wrong end," Grinnell laughed. "It *is* a radical departure from anything ever designed or built to date, I grant you, and it's causing quite a stir. Brown tells me there's already been spies snooping around from London. Let them snoop. This boat is going to be fast, real fast, and it will be a decade before they can build one like it."

Trask was stunned into silence by the majesty of the vessel, and Grinnell's unholy confidence.

"I've already named it, William, in your honor - the *Perseverance*." Grinnell turned his shoulders, and looked squarely at Trask. "I want you to captain this vessel, Trask, the proudest and fastest vessel on the oceans."

Grinnell had skillfully woven his golden web. Whereas Trask had come to this meeting to announce his retirement from the sea, Grinnell had successfully turned the affair in his favor to the point where now, it would appear to be the greatest of insults to decline Grinnell's heartfelt offer.

Trask felt suddenly dizzy. Perhaps it was the cigar, now smoked down to the nub, or perhaps it was the unassailable hardness of Grinnell's appeal that smacked him in the face. In any case, Trask had the distinct impression that Grinnell knew he felt dizzy, and had, in fact, planned on this very reaction, at this very moment, to successfully close this deal.

Trask found the strength to issue his reasoned response.

"Mr. Grinnell, this is the offer of a lifetime. It is an honor, and the confidence it displays in me is in a measure that I could never wholly justify, even should I sail successfully for you for the next 40 years. But I happen to know that there are nearly 30,000 vessels now sailing under the American flag with a capacity of over four million tons. Three hundred thousand seamen are required to sail these vessels, and their average sea-service is only 12 years. We are some of the most short-lived of men."

"William, I know you've had a hard time of it recently, but life goes on, and you're going to have to consider your livelihood. I don't have to tell you that there isn't much of a market for a one-legged former captain. There are 10,000 men on these piers who would trade their eye teeth for this opportunity. It's yours if you want it. Not because I admire you, which I do, but because you're the best damn captain of any vessel in any port. And the fact that you went down, *once*, hasn't changed that fact. You're still the best, and I want you on my ship."

Trask felt cornered, one-on-one, with the ablest negotiator in New York. The cheery warmth of the dinner table had now evaporated. Grinnell had turned ice-cold.

"Now think about it, William, and think about it hard. I won't say another word with you on this issue until Tuesday, which is when I need to hear your answer. Beyond that day, the offer is rescinded."

With that, he shook Trask's hand, and turned to walk home.

After Grinnell disappeared into the crowd, Trask limped out to the center of the street, and paused for a moment, surrounded by the crush of commercial life. He listened awhile to the hoarse orders of the landing as another vessel docked. He watched the dull-looking sailors pacing up and down the sidewalk, as if still on their watch on board. He heard in the distance the raucous din of the Cherry Street saloons, then followed the sound to find a room for the night.

FIRE ISLAND

Chapter Thirty-One

A Visit from Joshua James

"You've been gone for five days," Cassandra said upon seeing Trask at her door.

"I spent some extra time in New York getting to know the ol' docks again," Trask said, brushing by her.

"How's your leg?"

"Holding me up."

"I mean the other one."

"It's still not there," he said as he tumbled into an armchair. "And I still miss it."

"And Grinnell?" she asked, studying his face intensely.

"He wants me to captain for him again. He's building a beautiful new vessel, the *Perseverance*. Seven-hundred-and-fifty tons! It's supposed to be the fastest ship on the ocean, and he wants me to captain."

"What did you tell him?"

"I told him I was amazed at the vessel. I told him I was honored by the offer. I told him I would think about it."

Cassandra turned away from him for a moment, and Trask saw the feathery tufts of hair that cascaded gently from under her drawn-back hair gracing the soft white line of her neck. He wanted to kiss her right on that spot. Just sidle up to her from the back. Shock her. But he resisted the impulse.

"Cassandra, I really can't thank you enough for everything you've done."

"Don't mention it."

"If not for you, I'm sure I would have lost my life."

"It's my vocation. It's what I do. Some people take in stray cats and dogs. I take in shipwreck survivors."

"There you go, comparing me to cats and dogs. You really know the way to a man's heart."

"Mr. Trask, in case you haven't noticed, I'm not *trying* to make my way into your heart. Perhaps you think this is romantic: me, Florence Nightingale; you, the fallen hero. But let me remind you, I've tended to over 30 men thus far, most a sight more handsome than you."

"Miss Cassandra, stop," Dahlia said entering the room, carrying a freshly folded stack of linen in her arms. "The man hasn't been back in the house for five minutes, and already you're lecturing him. Hello, Mr. Trask. How *are* you?"

"Much better Dahlia, thank you."

"What Miss Cassandra has not told you, I'm sure, is that we had a visitor here this morning. A Mister Joshua James. He wants to speak with you."

"Joshua James?"

"He's the keeper of the new life saving station they're building at Lone Hill. I think it's a wonderful idea, and about time, too."

"What does he want with me?"

"He didn't say, but he did say he would be back this afternoon."

Just then there was a knock on the door. Dahlia answered it, and came back into the study.

"It's Mr. James."

Joshua James walked

Joshua James

stiffly into the study wearing the awkward uniform of the United States Lifesaving Service. The oversized keeper's cap was drawn low over his brow so that the visor shaded his eyes, his prickly full-length beard crowding out the other features on his face. Behind the gray-flecked beard, his mouth was pinned down permanently on both sides, and his chin jutted out in between giving the appearance of vigilance, courage and resolution.

Overall, he was a slight and small man who gave the impression that he was always standing up to a bully.

"Mr. Trask, it's my pleasure to meet you," James began, extending his hand. "I heard about your travail, and only regret that we weren't there at the time to be of some assistance. Our organization is newly formed, you see. We've just got a boat, and the station house is going up, even as we speak."

"Sit down, Mr. James," Dahlia said, seeing that Cassandra, lost in her thoughts, had neglected the invitation. "We'll put up some tea." With that she hustled Cassandra out of the study and into the kitchen.

James sat down, removed his cap, and placed it in his lap. He carried himself so formally, with such probity, that it was difficult not to be in awe.

"Mr. Trask, allow me to get right to the point," he began. "I know a lot about you. More than you know about me right now, I'm sure. And I know you can handle a boat. My men, they're good men, but I don't have a single boatman on the crew."

"How often do you go out?" Trask inquired.

"Once a week, on Saturdays,"

"I mean, to rescue."

"Well, it'll be a little while before storm season again. We'll find out then, I suppose."

"What is the pay?"

"Not much. And it's only for eight months, from October to May."

"Who'll captain?"

"I'm afraid that's my task," James said with assurance. "But you'll be one of my lead crewmen. I want you to help organize and run the drills, care for the boat, train the men. Make them sailors, if you can."

Dahlia and Cassandra came back into the study with the tea. Cassandra pretended not to listen to the conversation, though she was obviously concentrating intently on it. She poured the tea, spilling it badly on the serving tray. Dahlia dabbed it up with a rag, gently reprimanding Cassandra with her eyes.

"I must tell you, Mr. James. I've been recently offered the post of captain of the newest vessel from Grinnell & Fish Trading Company, the *Perseverance*. She's to sail the China trade."

"Our vessel is all of 23 feet," James chuckled. "And you won't be going very far. A mile or so out would be about the limit, I would guess..."

James' face suddenly became rock hard with resolution, and his eyes flashed. "The mission is a little different, 's'all."

It *had* always irked Trask that he sailed solely for commercial ventures. As a child, at the helm of the *Wharf Rat*, he had imagined voyages of adventure and conquest, but he had never thought that the purpose of these voyages would be to make money, and usually for someone else. Grinnell had always been a fair master, but he was a master nonetheless, and Trask's vocation of captain had always seemed tarnished by the purpose of his voyages - trade, commerce, capital acquisition. But his love of sailing had always carried him through.

"One caveat, though, Mr. Trask," James said, looking at him squarely. "My duty is to hire *able-bodied* seamen." Trask's insides froze. "There are some who might question whether a one-legged man is an able-bodied seaman." James paused for effect. Trask winced.

"I'm willing to put up with those questions, Mr. Trask, if you can prove to me you're able."

Cassandra was in the corner of the room, ostensibly fussing with a bouquet of flowers on the end table.

"It's quite an invitation," Trask said, feeling an odd sense of *deja vu*. "I'll consider it carefully."

"On Saturday, we will be commissioning the station house,"

James said, standing up suddenly to leave. "Why don't you stop by and see it, meet the crew. No obligation. Just look around."

"I just might, Mr. James."

"It won't hold the adventure that you're used to," James continued. "And it's plenty dangerous when a rescue is underway. But at least you stay put. You'll feel like you're a part of something. We can put you up at the station house when it's done, until you get a place of your own."

"Thanks again."

As he exited, James tipped his cap in the direction of Cassandra, still re-arranging the flowers.

"Ma'am..."

"Goodbye Mr. Grinnell," Cassandra said.

"That's *James*, ma'am. Joshua *James*."

FIRE ISLAND

Chapter Thirty-Two

Fire in the Mind

On the far wall of the library, the gold and orange reflections of a fire jig and twitch like an agonized spirit restrained from spiraling to heaven, condemned to attend to mortals on earth.

Gathered in a circle in the center of the room are seven members of the Transcendentalists Association, a group of artists, writers and philosophers in the area. Periodically they gathered to discuss the ideas espoused by Emerson: self-reliance, learning from Nature, and discerning the Word of God within oneself.

"...This is far too theoretical," said Cassandra, the only woman in the group. "Let us not forget that the goal is not to transcend the world. It is to engage ourselves fully in it. It is not principles that will distinguish this movement, but principles put into action."

A man rejoined.

"I commend you, Cassandra for everything you've done. And you are certainly an example to everything we stand for, but to each his own. Not everyone is capable of dramatic action in the world. Some are more suited to contemplative or artistic pursuits. Is not the creation of a work of beauty as fine a contribution to the well-being of mankind as the care of the sick and the poor?"

"Indeed, it may be more lasting," another man piped up.

"And what of those who perform good deeds in the world, but whose own souls are badly neglected? Would it not be better for this person to tend to himself first, save himself, before setting out to save the rest of mankind?"

"All very well and good, sitting around a warm fire, well-fed and among friends," said Cassandra, "but what of injustice in the world? What of seven-year-old children little better than slaves laboring 12-hours-a-day, six-days-a-week inside some hellish coal mine? What of the enslaved Negro? As long as property remains so wildly unequal those who possess it will live on the labor, distress and misery of others. Long have we borne this oppression in silence, but patience is no longer a virtue. Unredeemed soul or not, if we are not the grossest of hypocrites, must we not fight these evils with our hands? As well as our hearts, minds and souls?"

Her skin was luminous white appearing to reflect light from without and within. Fire leapt from her eyes which were defined by shallow circles comprised of skin of a darker pigmentation than the rest of her face. Here the muscles were taut and twitchy. Thin blue veins were apparent. These were the eyes of a woman in constant battle, these were eyes that had known great sadness, these were eyes that had known conflict, these were eyes that *knew*, there was a knowingness about them.

Emerson

After an uncomfortable pause, Emerson began "Cassandra, I really do believe that we live in the best of all possible worlds. And if there are things that to us seem to be injustices, I believe that with the perspective of God, these are temporary phenomenon that are working themselves out in their own due time. The Hand of God is relentlessly working its way through Time. Have faith that this force is working everything out for the best, even if we don't understand it, even if it takes a decade, a century, or a millenium to do so."

"Or a civil war..."

"Or a civil war. We are like travelers on a ship scurrying around the deck trying to reach our destination faster. The ship is moved by unseen forces - the wind, the current, the tides. The cosmos is the captain of our ships, the prime mover. The sooner we recognize that fact, the sooner we will be in harmony with it."

Cassandra turned her face to the fire now devolving into a hellish chamber of smoldering red embers. A slight puff of unseen air traveling over the fire rippled over the embers, flaring them momentarily from red to orange, then back to red again. His words seem to have the incontrovertible weight of authority.

"Mr. Emerson, I have nothing but the greatest respect for you and your work," Cassandra began. "Perhaps, you are right. There *are* many forms of action in the world. And perhaps I am short-changing the affect that the practice of art or philosophy has upon the world..."

"Artists are the legislators of the world," another man posited.

"And you, Mr. Hawthorne, sound like you are running for office," a third man shot back to a round of light laughter around the room.

"Now, gentlemen, Cassandra was just sharpening her point which was clearly aimed at me," Emerson said to re-focus the room. "Allow her to continue."

"Thank you, Mr. Emerson." Cassandra began again. "Perhaps we *have* set up a false demarcation between action in the world and contemplative pursuits. Surely, the practice of art, philosophy or pure science *is* of great and lasting value to the betterment of the world, but I ask you: if you were in your studio painting, and your seven-year-old son in the kitchen sliced his hand open with a knife, would you not immediately run to the kitchen to tend to the wound?

"Would you not leave your art, drop your paintbrush - in mid-stroke, if necessary - and run to the aid of your son?"

There was a flurry of reaction in the room...

"Cassandra, that's different."

"That analogy just doesn't hold up."

"What relationship does that have to injustice and suffering in the world?"

"I'm afraid it has all the relevance in the world," Cassandra responded. "The difference is the matter of urgency. When your son is wounded, it is your kin. There is no question, but that you should respond right away. Likewise, I suppose, if the person in distress is your neighbor. But the Negro? The woman denied access to education? The man turned into a machine by industry? The Chinaman in poverty? A sense of urgency seems to leave altogether. But, under God's dominion, we are *all* brothers and sisters. And we are hypocrites to play our parlor games of the mind while there is blood in the streets."

The passion and logic of her speech stunned the polite circle of friends. Her words rang true, but the unadorned directness of her presentation caused several in attendance to shift uneasily in their chairs.

It was left again to Emerson to rescue the conversation.

"Cassandra, I trust that we all count ourselves as your friends, and I might say, you wear your friends like a diamond necklace... And the fire in your mind makes each one of us shine a little brighter."

He looked around the room, and received a general nod of approbation.

"Tomorrow, on our walk, we will discuss this further," Emerson concluded.

Chapter Thirty-Three

The Mute Sea

With random power, the waves form the shoreline, re-form, mold a cove, overnight, add an inlet to the bay, erase this again with the next storm, carry immense tonnage of sand, grain by grain, from someplace to someplace, hiding the bulk of its handiwork beneath the gray-green, blue-black water - vast plains of undulating, pummeling water.

Trask slid to the side of the bed, and grabbed his crutch, hobbled and hopped his way out the door, and toward the water's edge. It was early evening, and, though he could not see the water just yet, he could hear the low rumbling roar it made as it routinely pounded the shoreline. It is a sound he had come to know very well. For three months now, as he regained his health, he heard the rhythmic chanting of the sea expunging itself on the sandy shore. One wave relentlessly following another.

At times, this brought him comfort, smothering with white noise the thoughts that crowded into his mind. At other times, the sound was wickedness itself, and each lunge of mighty ocean tonnage tore at the membrane of his soul riven as it already was by icy shards of memory.

Trask scampered up the side of a dune, and, standing atop it, beach grass about his one foot, he was stung into awe and wonder by the magnificence of the horizon. For months confined to a room, perhaps nine feet wide and 12 feet long, and now, *this*! A limitless vista! So broad, he could detect the curvature of the earth.

He looked back at the refuge house, propped upon a tiny promontory of sand and rock. Cassandra was in the front of the house helping Dahlia and Murray prop the huge timbers in a teepee-like construction for the first bonfire of the season.

Trask hobbled down off the dune, and trudged his way down to the water's edge. What was he hoping for? A greeting? It was strange to be reminded that the ocean was mute.

The energy that drives those waves swallowed Joshua, crushed the *Young America* to timbers, devoured its crew, and spit them out like refuse upon the shore. But it will not say a word - not one of penance, not one of shame, not one of reconciliation, not one of greeting.

Trask limped to the hard and wet sand made flat by the surf pummeling its way inexorably up the beach. He looked into the white foam frothing at the surface and, for a moment became mesmerized by the constantly changing hues - the pale green, steel gray, slate blue.

Then his eyes focused on the orange-red path of reflected light that led from the surf, out across the ocean, all the way to the sun itself, which, just now, was carving its heavy trajectory downward in the western sky.

The light jigged and twitched on the ocean surface. It oscillated with mercurial quickness. Where it is, it isn't, in an instant. Where it was, it is again, but different. Lightly it leapt from wavelet to wavelet existing wholly without substance. Like a diamond bridge leading into eternity, it beckoned with a dazzling beauty. 'Come,' it seemed to call, like Jesus inviting his apostles to walk upon the water.

A wave spent itself upon the beach, and wrapped around Trask's foot, waking him from his revelry. As the wave receded, it revealed a foot sunk in soft sand, and a crutch similarly encumbered. Trask tried to hop straight up to extract his foot, but succeeded only in falling over on his face into about three inches of wave water still fleeing back to the source.

Silly is how Trask felt at first, wriggling around in the wet sand like a turtle on its back. But the following wave wiped the smile from his face. Indeed, it covered his face completely. Of course! He has one leg now! He hadn't yet learned how little mobility he now has in the water. All those months in bed hadn't taught him. And it also occurred to him that no one knew where he was. He was out of earshot of everyone.

Another wave arrived, filling his mouth and nose with salt water. His crutch? Gone! Before the arrival of the next wave, Trask pulled himself a little further up the shoreline slope. But the following wave buried his head underwater again, and he came up gasping like a stuck seal. He tried to stand, but, before he could get on his foot, another wave hit him from behind, easily toppling him. The undertow sucked him out and under a little further.

Suspended in turbulence, there is nothing for him to hold onto; feeling for the bottom, there is none; reaching for the surface, it is not there. Open your eyes, there is nothing to see, but green-blackness. All the reliable methods of orientation are gone, even gravity. Breathe, and your lungs fill with water. The brain screams out for oxygen. Panic arrives, the mind's final grab for a horizon...

White foam seethed all around him. Somehow, Trask found the soft sand beneath him, and braced himself, still submerged, with his one foot, and waited for a moment. Just then a huge curl of water rose up, gathering strength from the rapidly depleting stand of water at the shoreline. Water being sucked into this muscular monster surged past his sunken foot at a frightening rate, yet somehow Trask maintained his position, waiting, waiting for the last possible moment when he would throw himself at the mercy of this surging fury.

At last, from within the very hollow of the wave, Trask leapt toward shore, arms forward, as the mighty wave collapsed all around him. He is rudely taken up, tumbling without gravitational reference, spinning head over heals, grasping for a fixed object until the back of his head is driven into the sand.

When the wave draws back, Trask immediately pulls himself over the sand with his arms, and pumps awkwardly with his leg. The follow-up wave is weak affording him a chance to inch closer to the dry sand.

There, Trask turns over, exhausted from his efforts, his chest heaving wildly.

"Oh god," he utters between breaths.

There would be no mercy from the mute sea for William I. H. Trask. He looked back toward Cassandra's house, and realized he needed help.

Chapter Thirty-Four

Commission of the Station House

"Welcome," James said loudly to the assembled crowd gathered in the sand around the new station house. Everyone quickly settled into a quiet state of attention.

"Welcome, to the United States Lifesaving Station #1 at Lone Hill. By the way, please do stay around after the ceremonies. There will be tours of the station, and a clambake on the beach, and some *fireworks* tonight."

There was a slight smattering of applause. Surrounding the station in the sandy dunes of the upper beach, were some 60 people from the mainland, friends and relatives of the surfmen and the curious. William Trask was among them, leaning on his crutch in the back, flanked by Cassandra and Dahlia. Frank Eck was there, nattily-dressed, looking like the morning after.

"There are so many people who helped in making this day possible, but most especially Charles Howard, who donated the land."

Howard waved his hand in the air to the receipt of light applause.

James continued. "There are some as is doomed to die; and some that are not. Such as are, will die; such as not, we will save. It's our day's work, and the men will do their mighty best."

The crowd applauded, and Trask found himself blinking back little pools of water that suddenly filled his eyes.

"Our mission here is clear: Duty, a sense of obligation, and the credit we can bring to this community and the Service."

With that, James gestured to his right where a small military band had been waiting. The conductor raised his hand, and the band began to play "Do They Miss Me At Home."

The surfmen, as dutifully ordered by James, formed a small choir, and sang along:

> *When twilight approached the season*
> *That ever is sacred to song*
> *Does some one repeat my name over*
> *And sigh that I tarry so long*
> *And is there a chord in the music*
> *That's missed when my voice is away*
> *And a chord in each heart that awaketh*
> *Regret at my wearisome stay*
> *Regret at my wearisome stay.*

As rehearsed, Elijah Slocum then ceremoniously marched, with folded flag in hand, to the tall white staff that stood erect at the side of the station house, and slowly ran the United States flag, complete with 31 stars, up into the pale blue sky.

With the musical rendition ended, James pulled on a line rigged to a sheet that covered the transom over the barn doors. The sheet peeled back, and fell to the ground revealing the newly minted logo of the United States Lifesaving Service, a lifebuoy crossed with a boat oar and a grappling hook, carved into a headboard on the front upper portion of the station house.

The crowd cheered at the unveiling.

"And now," James began again, "I will call the name of each member of Station #1, and they will walk up, and receive their order of rank. As they come up, please do keep

in mind that the thought of mercenary reward has never once entered the minds of these men who have joined the service..."

"Maybe it never entered *his* mind," Jimmy Gilbert cracked quietly to Thomas Mannering standing by his side.

"Elijah Slocum..."

"Jeremiah Slocum..."

"Jimmy Gilbert..."

As each man's name was barked out by Joshua James, they walked up the boat ramp with the degree of solemnity that each could muster to receive his own official uniform and shield with his order of rank stitched on it. James stood at the head of the ramp in front of the large barn doors that faced the sea of the newly-built lifesaving station.

"Joseph Murphy..."

"Thomas Mannering..."

"Abraham Century..."

When Abraham Century approached, James decorously handed him the shield with the number *one* on it establishing him as the lead crewmen at the station house. From that moment on, he was to be the unequivocal leader among the men.

The townspeople then lined up to file through the building on a tour. The station house was a modest structure, little more than a shed to house the boat, with some Spartan living area for the crew. It was an A-frame chalet-like structure, 42 feet in length by 18 feet wide with cedar shingles on its roof and sides. It was built on poles to raise it off the beach in case of storm tide flooding. Thick wooden shutters hung on 18-inch wrought iron trap hinges protected the windows on the main and upper floor. The roof was painted red so as to be more visible to sailors off Fire Island. It had an open platform built crudely into it as a lookout.

The gutters under the roof eaves led to a cistern that served as the crew's source of fresh water. A small outbuilding contained the privy.

On the ground floor, two-thirds of the space was given over to the *Audacious*. The townspeople walked around it as if it were a holy object. Over the transom, the men had hung the name plate of the three-masted schooner *Louis V. Place*, a relic of a wreck. Off to one side, was a basic kitchen with a stove, sink and large table. There was a small wooden tub for the Saturday night bath positioned next to the fire, the only source of warm water and heat.

Those who were curious then climbed a wooden ladder in the corner, and peeped their heads through a round opening into the loft which was divided into rooms for the keeper and crew, and for storage.

Trask was one who went up, more so as a test for himself, to see if, indeed, he could climb a ladder with one leg. He laid his crutch aside, brushing off an on-looker who wanted to help. He grabbed both sides of the ladder with his hands, and hopped his leg up to the first rung. So far, so good. Each succeeding rung was more difficult because, rather than hop his leg upwards, he had to lift it out, up and around, suspending his entire body weight each time with his arms. First he would kneel, then he would stand. Lift - kneel - lift - stand, lift - kneel - lift - stand, all the way to the top. James, standing like a soldier on guard at the open barn doors, watched the entire affair out of the corner of his eye. Everyone else watched as well, in silent discomfort, not knowing what to say or do.

Trask made it to the top, and peered around the upstairs quarters from the top run of the ladder. Lowering his body down rung-by-rung required perhaps even greater upper body strength. But Trask managed, with some difficulty, and a certain degree of shame. At the base of the ladder again, he reached for his crutch, panting heavily.

The clambake was a festive affair, with the military band now transformed into a music box, played "The Old Folks at Home," by Stephen Foster.

Everyone sang along.

> *Way down upon de Swanee ribber,*
> *Far, far away,*

Dere's wha my heart is turning ebber,
Dere's wha de old folks stay.

All up down de whole creation,
Sadly I roam,
Still longing for de old plantation,
And for de old folks at home.

All de world am sad and dreary,
Eb'ry where I roam,
Oh! darkeys how my heart grows weary,
Far from de old folks at home.

All round de little farm I wandered When
I was young,
Dem many happy days I squandered,
Many de songs I sung.

When I was playing wid my brudder
Happy was I.
Oh! take me to my kind old mudder,
Dere let me live and die.

Embers glowed from within a deep hole in the beach, ideal for a barbecue. Eck and his cronies hung around the outskirts of the crowds, eating more than their share, and slurping from a whiskey flask that they passed around greedily. A huge bonfire with flames leaping 20-feet into the air lit the scene, and provided heat as the evening chill came quickly and without remorse at sundown.

After the modest fireworks display, the band packed up, and bit by bit, the evening called away little groups of people. As the crowd dwindled, the sound of the ocean seemed to re-fill the space. It seemed immensely large, suddenly, as if it had receded entirely for those few hours, and now had simply risen again, like a tide, to loom large again in the minds of those who remained.

Trask sat on a log by the fire. Next to him sat Cassandra, then Dahlia. All three were wrapped together in a blanket provided by one of the surfmen from the station house.

Earlier in the evening, Trask had had too much to drink. Now, he felt fagged out and sober, like the smoky burnt end of a poker stick. He had clearly kept Cassandra and Dahlia there too long. But Cassandra could see the coiled workings of his soul, unwinding itself out and around the event. Trask was trying on the place, like someone putting on a new shoe.

"*Is this a bed I could sleep on?*" she could see him thinking. "*Are these the walls I could look at for years? Are these the people who I could share the better part of my new life? Is this my new horizon?*"

She was determined to stay all night, if she had to, in order for him to answer those questions.

"Miss Cassandra, I really am very cold," Dahlia said gently. She had been watching Abraham Century all night, but now she was tired even of that. "And it *is* a long walk back to the house. Feel free to stay, if you like, but I'm going to head back, and get a fire going for the night."

"Oh course, Dahlia," Cassandra responded. "Thank you for coming."

"Cassandra, why don't you head back as well," Trask piped up from his funk. "I need to speak with Mr. James."

"OK," Cassandra said gently, her head inclining toward his shoulder.

"I'll be fine," he responded with a little squeeze of her hand.

With that, they parted, the two ladies marching off into the darkness. Trask watched them off for a moment.

"Murray, be a good man, and see them back to the house," Trask said, and gestured to him to follow. Murray obliged, and soon caught up with them.

Trask then hobbled up the ramp to see Joshua James, still standing, oddly, at the opening to the station house, looking out into the ocean.

A fat harvest moon was rising skyward as if it were lighter than air, the shadows on its facade looking like a Jack-O-Lantern cackling hysterically. The glistening light bridge the moon projected onto the water reached all the way from it to the beach, looking like a path of silver fireworks leading to eternity. The reflections danced in James' eyes, animating his otherwise vacant expression. He looked like a scarecrow, not quite alive, not quite dead.

"I have something for you," James said by way of greeting without averting his eyes from the ocean. He reached into a satchel, and withdrew another shield. It had the number *seven* on it.

"Welcome to the United States Lifesaving Service, Station No. 1 at Lone Hill, Fire Island. Your bunk is upstairs. We can send for your things tomorrow. Breakfast is 0:700. First drill is 0:800."

Trask was stunned by the resolution in his voice. It had been a good 10 years since he had taken an order.

"Aye, aye, sir," Trask said as he hobbled past James into the darkened hut.

"Trask," James called back into the hut, "right now, you're the low man on the totem pole...I don't expect that to last."

"Aye, sir."

Grinnell would just have to find another captain, Trask thought as he lay in his bunk for the first time. There were plenty of them, he assured himself, being born every day.

FIRE ISLAND

JOHN J. STEVENS

Chapter Thirty-Five

Fire in the Heart

Cassandra opened the storm door to her cottage, and entered through the kitchen into the living room. She undraped her overcoat, and slumped into the soft chair by the fire. Murray busied himself to light a fire. He prided himself on few things. Lighting a quick fire was one of them. Rummy grabbed his spot on the floor by the fireplace. Dahlia, now dressed in her night clothes, soon joined them. She pulled up the rocker, and opened her bible.

"The *weend* is wicked outside, j's wicked," she offered. "Ecclesiates will keep me busy though. 'O vanity of vanities, all is vanity.'"

"Dahlia, I'd love to engage you in some lively discussion, but I'm all talked out tonight."

Cassandra's eyes drifted up over the fireplace to the mantel above.

A modest candle just lit burned thereupon. A small spiff of air fluttered the flame point, causing it to twist awkwardly for a moment emitting a wispy spoof of black smoke twisting into the air above it.

Settling again into a stiller state, the candle flame emitted a golden halo of light which illuminated the haunting image of a handsome man framed upon the wall over the mantel.

His head was cocked slightly to the right, with a workingman's hat tilted rakishly to the same side. His full mustache bristled out beyond his lips, then drooped down on either side to form a trim beard on his chin. His eyes possessed an uncommon gaze in this image. The pupils seemed chiseled into a perfect circle with radiant gray spokes leading to a very wide iris. There was a thoughtful intelligence resident in this man's face that mitigated the hard angles of his facade.

As the light from the flame danced across the image, it seemed as if the face of this man would move. It took a force of effort not to stare back into his eyes.

Dahlia recognized Cassandra's odd trance.

"'Tis an evil lot to have a man's ambition, and a woman's heart," Dahlia said.

Cassandra stared into the heart of the flame, the inner flame, blue hot with intensity.

"I wonder where he is now," Cassandra began with uncharacteristic introspection. "Is he...*anywhere*? Is he who he was before he died? Is he conscious of who he is, or was? Does he still know who I am? Does he remember...us?"

Dahlia lifted herself from the chair, rumbled across the room to stand behind Cassandra, and said: "The LORD puts to death, and gives life; he casts down to the nether world; he raises up again. The LORD makes poor, and makes rich, he humbles, he also exalts."

Then she began tenderly to twist and untwist large hunks of Cassandra's hair. Her large black hands worked their way underneath to her scalp, and began to pull her hair up and out from her head. She groomed Cassandra's hair straight back over her head, and began to massage her scalp line. Cassandra surrendered to the strength in her hands.

She remembered that feeling of surrender, with Lochlan one evening - she remembered feeling completely overwhelmed by him; she reached for his upper arm, and felt muscle – a taut force, poised for effort. He brought himself down into her, and she let out a little hurt murmur – sounding, as this little resistance left her mouth, like a schoolgirl. He felt so heavy – she could hardly breathe – and the smell of him was suffocating. She writhed for a bit, but then…a little toggle inside her was thrown. She gave up – and relaxed herself into him completely. If she were to be hurt, she would be hurt. If she were to be crushed, she would be crushed.

But she was *not* hurt, *not* crushed. She was *loved* – by a man whom *she* loved. His arm worked its way behind her neck, and something like lightening worked its way through her lower body…

"They saying now that you can read a person by the bumps on thay head," Dahlia proclaimed.

"Oh," Cassandra murmured with her eyes half-closed, "and what does my head say about me?"

"You? Le'me see…"she said, feeling her way around the crown of her head. "Near as I can tell, you've got rocks in yo' head, woman!"

Dahlia's laughter tumbled out in huge paroxysms of glee. It tore through the melancholy of the night like a radiant sword. The wind itself seemed to howl in sympathetic response. Her laughter was vengeance and power itself, frightening hobgoblins back to their corners. Peal after peal it kept coming, like waves upon the shore, until Cassandra could no longer contain herself, and joined in. Soon, they both had tears in their eyes, and were holding onto each other like long-lost sisters. For some few blessed moments, all self-consciousness had left them both. They were free and happy.

After a good long time, the laughter subsided, resurfacing in spurts of little sobbing fits, like aftershocks of an earthquake. Finally, the two women were spent, together in the chair - Cassandra on the cushion, and Dahlia on the armrest.

The dance of the fire, the glow from the candle flame, the howling of the wind, the strange and steady gaze of the man in the picture…these remained.

Cassandra leaned her head onto Dahlia's bosom. Emotion overcame her, and she began to cry…

Murray paced back and forth hurriedly in cramped three-foot increments occasionally snatching a quick look at Cassandra crying, looking down again quickly, unbearably embarassed by her tears, afraid to leave, afraid to stop pacing, afraid to look, afraid not to, as if late for an appointment, an appointment he couldn't remember, interminable motion, going nowhere, until Cassandra could no longer take it.

"Murray, why don't you sleep in the front room?" she offered.

"O'owt, nthere," he said, and slipped out into the night without saying anything more, Rummy trailing close behind.

Chapter Thirty-Six

The Association Meeting

Grinnell walked into the room as if he owned it. He learned that from his father "Enter a king," he told the young Moses. It would be a hard trick to pull off in this room, stacked as it was with a stern gaggle of some of the most powerful merchants in lower New York.

These were men who had amassed fortunes the likes of which the world had not previously known. Some, like Cornelius Vanderbilt, had done so through ruthless intensity. Some, like Jay Gould, had done so through cunning. Diamond Jim Fisk did so through market speculation. They were the governors of the nation's wealth.

The appointments in this room could be intimidating: soft black imported leather backed chairs, a 24-foot-long polished redwood conference table, at each place crystal goblets filled with ice water, paper and fine writing implements for notes.

Grinnell exchanged pleasantries with a few men standing in discreet clusters around the room. Miniturn was candid. Chaplain was cold. Vanderbilt tried to conceal the paranoid darting side-to-side of his eyes.

Miniturn politely tapped the gavel at the head of the table, and the meeting came to order.

"Gentlemen, gentlemen. The meeting of the New Amsterdam Merchant's Society is now officially called to order!

"Mr. Secretary, please call the roll!"

"Mr. Ambose."
"Here!"
"Mr. Boxwood."
"Here!"

Enter a King

One by one the names of the builders of the burgeoning American Empire confirmed their presence.

Indeed, Grinnell's company was one of the smaller firms represented in the room. After the reading of the minutes from the last meeting, Miniturn began.

"Tonight, we're to get a report from Mr. Grinnell on the progress of the United States Lifesaving Service. Grinnell."

Moses rose from his seat.

"As you know, Senator Callaghan has seen fit to shepherd legislation through the Congress that has enabled funding for the creation of the United States Lifesaving Service.

"At the request of this organization, the release of funds has been expedited, and progress is moving forward apace. The first four station houses have been built on Fire Island, and plans for 13 additional station houses have been drawn up.

"The prototype lifesaving vessels, designed and built by a member of this organization, William Webb, have been delivered on-site. Indeed, lifesaving drills using the boat are underway, and have met with great results. The Webb shipyard has proven its mettle once again."

Polite clapping rippled around the room.

"The station houses have been manned and outfitted. The station keepers have been chosen. The practice drills have begun, through from what I understand, the early results have not been encouraging.

"I don't need to remind the esteemed members of this august body of the importantce of this endeavor. It is long overdue, and will soon aid in the recovery of the goods and crew aboard these vessels. Commerce will soon be more secure, and the safety of our crews more assured than ever."

More applause.

"We have to thank for this effort our congressman Henry Callaghan who is also our special guest this evening."

Callaghan nodded his head, and smiled around his table and the room. "Mr. Callaghan as you know was instrumental in securing the appropriation for this effort. He energized his colleagues, introduced the measure, and saw it through to signing by the president with a strong and steady hand."

Hearty applause followed all around, and Callaghan gallantly stood and bowed.

"In appreciation of this effort, the New Amsterdam and Merchants Association has collected $10,000 in support of Mr. Callaghan's next campaign."

With that, Senator Callaghan was presented with a bank's check from the First Bank of New York.

FIRE ISLAND

Chapter Thirty-Seven

Trask Leaves Cassandra's Care

Trask tapped gently at Cassandra's door. It is still early, perhaps too early. He had come back for his belongings, though they weren't much.

The door opened a crack, and Dahlia's face filled the gap. Her hair was not tied off in its usual blue and white kerchief, and it sprung out in every direction. Her skin seemed washed-out, lighter than usual, a soft chalky brown, like beach clay dried in the sun. It was obvious she had just woken up. But for Trask, seeing her undone like this was like seeing her for the very first time. She was beautiful. And in the late morning sun, the colors in her face were radiant - browns and yellows and greens, pinks, even blue.

"Good morning, Mr. Trask," she said as cheerfully as she could manage. "I'm afraid M's Cassandra is still asleep j's now."

"Who is it, Dahlia?" came Cassandra's voice from inside the house.

"Oh, it's Mr. Trask!" Dahlia shouted back.

A pause.

"Have him wait in the front room."

"Yes, ma'am."

Dahlia shrugged a little as she ushered Trask, now in his ill-fitting wool uniform, like a new guest into a house he had lived in for three months.

"What a *handsome* uniform," Dahlia admired.

"I like yours, too," Trask wisecracked, seeing that Dahlia was still in her nightgown. Obviously, he was feeling better.

Dahlia gave him a playful slap on the shoulder, and Trask noticed the outline of her body through the sheer material as she sauntered up the stairs to change.

Alone in the front room now, the unease Trask felt upon entering only increased as he waited upon Cassandra's arrival. He felt like a 15-year-old boy on his first date, fidgeting nervously with the sleeves of his jacket. The house looked so different from this perspective. The light from the rising sun streaked across the room, and illuminated the bookshelves on the far side. They were neatly stuffed with volumes of philosophy and history, Greek and Roman classics, Plato, Seneca, Aristotle, Euripides. It was filled with the objects that Cassandra and Dahlia loved.

Cassandra's reading glasses were on the night table next to her chair. Trask suddenly imagined Cassandra, during all those agonizing nights he spent in pain in the bedroom, sitting in this chair by the fire, reading, falling asleep, waking to tend to him and Arnold, reading and falling asleep again.

"Hello, William," Cassandra said upon entering. She extended her hand - rather formally Trask thought, considering that this same woman had bathed him when he was unable, assisted in the amputation of his leg, and many times changed the linen on his bed.

"Hello, Cassandra," Trask replied. "I was just admiring your house."

"I'm glad you've noticed," she replied.

"I've come back for my things," Trask began, rather stiffly. "I've joined the lifesaving service."

"I *see*," she said, looking him over with exaggerated admiration. "Would you like some tea?"

"I'd love to, but I have to be back at drills at 2 o'clock."

"You've got plenty of time. Sit down, please. Dahlia, would you be so kind as to make us some tea."

"Yes, ma'am," came Dahlia's singsong response from inside the house.

"Sleep well at the station house?" Cassandra ventured.

"I didn't sleep at all, actually. Too wound up. I couldn't shut my mind off."

"What was troubling you?"

"Everything...and nothing, all at the same time."

Cassandra raised an eyebrow from behind her clasped hands.

"James seems to be a fair taskmaster," Trask continued, his voice falling away. Cassandra's silent gaze encouraged him to go on. "Now I'm low man on the totem pole."

"Life doesn't always go in a straight line, William," she said gently. "It's round, 360-degrees. And the universe has a lot of strange surprises in store for us. A lot of turns in the road. I was going to be an editor, a college professor. But when Lochlan died...I didn't fall to the bottom of the barrel, I fell out of the barrel itself."

"I can tell how much you loved him."

"It wasn't that I loved him, I did." That old feeling welled up in Cassandra's throat, and threatened to swamp her. She forced it back. "It was that he loved me. And the *way* that he loved me."

Cassandra could see a shadow pass across Trask's face. It was clearly bad form to talk about another man this way in a man's presence, even if that other man is your dead husband. She had shared too much, revealed too much of herself.

Dahlia eased the tension just then by arriving with the tea.

"That's two lumps for Mr. Trask?"

"Yes, Dahlia. Thank you for remembering."

"Please forgive me for burdening you with such talk," Cassandra said finally after her first sip of tea had braced her. "I hadn't expected the conversation to go in this direction. I'm sorry."

"It's quite all right. I know how it is to lose someone you love."

"Oh, that reminds me," Cassandra perked up, standing. "Josh's logbook." She walked out, and returned with a large satchel. "It's at the bottom of the bag. I threw in some blankets for you as well. You're going to need them."

How did she know to pack his things, he wondered?

"You've been so kind, Cassandra," Trask replied, raising himself up clumsily from the table, and standing directly in front of her. "There is no way I could ever return this kindness to you in equal measure."

Cassandra could feel herself being drawn into his chest. She turned her head, and pressed it hard against the coarse wool of his pullover. The top of her head merely reached the bottom of his chin, and she felt completely enveloped in his arms. Involuntarily, she drew a long breath, and filled herself with his scent. She felt relaxed and safe. She squeezed him tightly. But she dared not raise her head.

For his part, Trask leaned over her a bit, using her to keep himself from falling over.

He hopped once or twice for balance, and felt the strength in her hands and arms.

He had expected an embrace at parting when he came by on this morning. He just didn't expect it to linger like this. They seemed to hover together, apart from time and space, locked in each other's arms, with nowhere to go but onward...

Trask felt the softness of her hair on his cheek. He closed his eyes for a moment, and savored the feel of her burrowed into his chest.

Cassandra felt that same sweet pang of loss, hitting her like a punch to the gut, the one she always felt when she thought of Lochlan. *He* had left like this, too. He had hugged her at the door. He had surrounded her with his arms. He, too, had smelled like home, and looked at her softly with his eyes...

She released her hold, and withdrew, keeping her head down for a moment as she reached for Trask's satchel.

"Mr. Trask," she said, looking up at him bravely as she handed him his things, "you are now well. Go back into the world from whence you came." Her words had a finality to them that she hadn't intended.

"And don't forget *me*," Dahlia said laughing as she bustled up to him for a big hug. "Now, Mr. Trask, every Saturday, we have an early dinner before the meeting. You're invited this Saturday, right Miss Cassandra? I'm making a chicken soup. And my chicken soup is worth coming by for. You know that. Don't miss it!"

"Thank you for the invitation," Trask said as he exited the door.

"I'm expecting you," Dahlia said calling after him. "Don't let me down now..."

With the door safely closed, Cassandra slumped into her favorite chair in the front room. The light from the window burned a crosshatch pattern onto the burnished floor. Dust particles, like little lost white angels, drifted aimlessly through the light. Cassandra watched them curiously as they floated, suspended in time. Then she waved her hand through the air, and looked on as the turbulence swept them up, and carried them off somewhere into the darker corners of the room.

FIRE ISLAND

Chapter Thirty-Eight

Sabotage

"I don't like what I'm seeing, I don't like it." Eck said, pacing in his tiny room, looking for something he couldn't find. Every nook and cranny of Eck's ramshackle houseboat was overstuffed with debris.

"You said this tea would keep us flush," Supercargo Butler whined. "You said we had plenty of money."

"They're going to put us out of business, Butler," Eck shouted. "Can't you see that? Where is that thing, dammit!"

Eck Aboard the Sister Vincent

Eck paced through each room of the houseboat keeping his head low as he went. The vessel was a comical affair. He had built it himself without plans, and it looked it. Over the years, he had constructed additions of various shapes, sizes and colors, usually from the flotsam and jetsam washed up by the surf. At one point, he came upon a homemade raft that had washed up on the bay side of Fire Island. He lashed it to starboard, and hastily constructed some walls and a roof to cover the deck from lumber he had stripped from the *Ayshire*. That became his bedroom complete with garish pink curtains, which he had picked up off of the wreck of the *Santa Domingo*. On the side of the boat, slapdashed crudely with white paint that had dripped well before it had dried, was the name of the vessel, *Sister Vincent*.

"The station house was bad enough. But now they've got this Lyle gun. Do you know what this thing can do?" he said, not expecting an answer. Eck broke through some hanging curtains into the "front room" as he sarcastically referred to it. This was so stuffed with cases of tea that he could barely turn around in it.

"Six hundred yards, they're saying. SIX-HUNDRED-YARDS! That's good enough for most wrecks. They could unload 'em without getting their toes wet!"

He ran up a wooden gangway, also stolen from a wreck, into the second story of this monstrosity, and kept up his harangue to Butler and Joe the Indian, who sat lolling with his eyes half-closed.

"This place is driving me crazy!" Eck screamed, after something upstairs came crashing off it perch.

"Butler, give me a hand, will ya'?"

"I can't hear you, boss," Butler yelled toward the ceiling, while he exchanged a smirk with Joe the Indian.

"I'm staying right here," Supercargo Butler whispered to Joe as he stretched his socked toes toward the potbellied stove. "Not moving a muscle."

"I hear they're going to demonstrate this damn thing on the beach," Eck continued. "They shoot it at a pole in the sand with some fake crosstrees. It's powerful, I can tell you, the real thing."

"I still can't *hear* you," Supercargo Butler yelled toward the ceiling. Joe was beside himself with glee.

"But I've got an idea, men. I've always got an idea...If I could only *find* the damn thing."

The floorboards creaked as Eck continued scurrying above.

"Aha!" Eck exclaimed. "I see it!" More debris crashed floorward. "Now, to get it...Butler, I need you. Now!!!"

Supercargo Butler jumped off his chair, and scampered up the gangway.

When the two men come down, they are carrying a large metal flask meant for carrying water, a good two gallons of it at a time.

"Gunpowder hates water, men. Where there is water, there are no fireworks."

The hideous sound of Eck's cackle filled the room.

"But they're after people, Eck," Joe piped up. "We're not in'r'sted in people."

"Don't believe it. They'll be divvying up the goodies as soon as the crowd goes home. What do you think they're doing this for? They're working on a government salary!!"

Joe took another hit of his whiskey.

"Listen, I know how people think. They go into it all high-minded, but once there's goodies on the table, they'll be stuffing them in their pockets when no one's looking. It's human nature. You can't change that."

Supercargo Butler stretched his toes toward the heat, and rolled them around in his new woolen socks.

"Now, I happen to know where they are keeping this Lyle gun, and where they keep the powder. While you people were having your laughs at the commissioning, I was snooping around. During the next storm, Joe you're going to slip into the shed next to the main house, and pee on their powder, so to speak."

"Huh?" Joe sat up with a lugubrious look on his face. "Why me, Eck?"

"Because you're the sneaky one, Joe. You could sneak up on a raccoon at night in the woods."

Joe felt a strange bristling of pride, and sat back again. There was no point in resisting, he thought to himself, might as well just go along, and see what happens.

"Now, for a toast!" Eck announced, feeling better about things. "To the fine art of sabotage," he said, raising the dented tin cup that served as his cocktail glass. "This is going to be fun, boys, a whole lot of fun."

FIRE ISLAND

Chapter Thirty-Nine

Trask Joins the Service

The first sign Trask saw of the lifesaving station upon his return was the flagpole. Upon it were the colors of the U.S. flag, kicking with life from the brisk afternoon breeze coming off the surf. Little flicks of sand pummeled his leg as the wind wrapped itself around him. Reef, the loopy Newfoundland mascot at the station house, lunkered down the beach to greet him, a happy tail propelling in a wide arc behind him. He dutifully trotted alongside Trask as his escort, and in keeping with what the loyal companion considered a solemn responsibility, a grave look was maintained upon his face.

As Trask came around another group of dunes, he saw the bright red roof of the station house, and the small exposed lookout that had been hastily added onto the roof at James' request. The October light striking the facade of the facility was

Reef

white, crisp and clean.

Trask heard the sound of a fiddle with rhythmic hands clapping coming from inside the station house.

Just then, exiting from the outhouse with the half-moon upon the door was Abraham Century, his white shirt billowing off his solid frame. Reef ran ahead to get his attention.

"Mr. Century!" Trask called out. "William Trask, reporting for duty."

"We thought we lost you," Century replied.

"Well, I've come back to see if my bed really was as hard as I thought it was last night."

Four miles there and four miles back, exposed to the sun and wind, his crutch oozing into the soft sand at every step, Trask suddenly felt exhausted. Century relieved Trask of the burden of his belongings.

"I'll get you some water," Century offered.

Century jogged up ahead, and scooped a tin full of water out of the rain barrel. Trask greedily gulped it down, the excess spilling out of the sides of his mouth, and down his chin.

Century plodded heavily to the station house with Trask loping along on his crutch behind him. There, some of the off-duty surfmen had gathered in the mess-room. In the corner, on a stool, Skull Murphy tore into his fiddle, coaxing from it layer upon layer of sound, emanating in ever-widening and repeatable waves. Thomas Mannering worked some coarse cord into an elaborate chain of fine ringlets, each stitched carefully into the others, extending outward, like Murphy's music, into space in an endlessly repeatable pattern. Elijah and Jeremiah Slocum listlessly played checkers at the table.

"Gentlemen, you know William Trask," Century announced brusquely. "He's our new man, now. Number seven."

Each of the men present introduced themselves. Mannering shook his hand.

"Come with me," Century said, and lead the way through the back of the station house, down a rough path through the dune brambles laden with beach plums. A clutch of caged chickens clucked with self-important fussiness as they approached the small shed in the hollow of a group of dunes.

"It's the chicken coop. You're responsible for keeping it clean, and in good working order."

"Chickens? I don't know anything about chickens."

"I don't either."

Century flashed an enigmatic smile, then trudged away in the sand.

As Trask looked after him, the strangeness of these events closed in around him like fog smothering a harbor. Gone, was the unlimited horizon of a ship's captain. Gone, was the golden glow of ultimate possibility in which he had indulged for the three months of his recuperation. Trask's world had become small, real. The grand miracle had calcified into concrete reality.

Trask looked down at the supercilious chickens strutting around for show. They seemed content in their home, busying themselves with nothing, chasing and prodding each other all day long.

"Bock, bock, bock-OCK..." Trask made a funny clucking sound in imitation of the chickens.

"Bock, bock, bock-OCK..."

An afternoon breeze freshened across the green-bearded dunes. Trask looked out toward the ocean horizon.

Like a greedy hand, forever grasping what it can, and drawing it into its insatiable self, not caring whether it be shell or stone or sand or a man and his wooden boats. Like an ancient and cryptic language, it lingers just outside the boundaries of comprehension. Unknowable. Forever.

FIRE ISLAND

Chapter Forty

Her Walk With Emerson

"Let's walk today where there *are* no paths," Emerson said to Cassandra Wolff as they veered off the regular trail, and into the woods...

These northeastern woods in mid-October stung the eyes with their richness of color - burnt oranges, reds honed by the sun, dappled with black, golds powered by the hand of God. Air, lightly toasted, rippled through the upper reaches of majestic trees, fanning in sequence the crisply colored leaves. It was a profusion of riches spilling out shamelessly without economy or governance.

"It is *so* beautiful," Cassandra said, compelled to state what was so obvious. "I can't believe how beautiful it truly is."

"It goes beyond words," Emerson replied, equally awestruck. "Indeed, Cassandra, I'd like us to try something. Let us try just walking together without talking at all. Through the woods, with no path, without speaking, surrounded by God's beauty."

Cassandra couldn't say *no* though it seemed uncomfortable at first, too intimate, to walk with a man - not your brother or your betrothed - alone in the woods without speaking. But this strange feeling was soon purged by the irresistible force of beauty that pushed in on them from every side.

After a time, they even held hands, and Cassandra was charged with an electric thrill of release. She felt like she was eight-years-old, in the hands of a mythical, gentle father who cared for her deeply, and only wanted to share with her his joy of being alive. Every step Emerson took reflected this joy, and his eyes twinkled with the dappled reflections of God's light through the leaves...

They followed the sound of water, and soon came upon a rocky brook dancing carelessly down the side of the hill. They sat there upon the largest stone.

"Have we had enough of silence?" he looked at her with a smile.

"Yes. It was nice, though," Cassandra replied sweetly.

"Did you hear God's voice?" he said, looking away.

Cassandra was stunned by his question. "I'm not sure I know what you mean."

"It's only in silence, in the presence of God's beauty, can we truly hear God's voice."

Emerson let the silence fill up the space between them again. That strange uncomfortable sense of intimacy rose up in Cassandra's stomach again. She was suddenly aware of how alone she was with him, out in the woods, outside of even earshot of another human being. She gathered herself.

"But how do you recognize the Voice of God in your heart?" she asked. "How is it different from any other sort of prompting?"

"Say, for earthly love, perhaps?"

"Perhaps."

Emerson shifted his weight before answering. "I believe God doesn't place Desire in one's heart, unless he has provided one with the intention, and the means of pursuing it. I don't believe in trying to extinguish Desire, as some of my friends from the East do. I believe Desire *is* the Voice of God."

Watching the stream, he let that sink in a moment.

"But your question is: how do we distinguish this desire from some passing fancy?"

Emerson brushed a rude bee away from his face.

"Hah! See! Everything happens for a reason." He was suddenly amused. "We may get stung on our walk today, and the itch may last a day or two. But God's sting lasts forever, and the itch doesn't go away until we fulfill the desire or die in its pursuit."

Cassandra felt the entire world coalesce around this odd man. He had clearly struck gold, a nugget of profound substance and value.

"*That* is how you recognize the Voice of God," he said, finally looking straight at her. "It's a sting that itches forever."

FIRE ISLAND

Chapter Forty-One

The Introduction of the Lyle Gun

"This is it, I tell you. This is it! They've tried hot air balloons. They've tried kites and rockets. They've even tried Aiken's cannon. What a notion! The idea was to shoot the *cannon itself* to the ship! Of course, in that case, if you miss, there goes your canon! Ha! I guess old Aiken hadn't thought it through!"

Words rumbled out of Captain Douglas Ottinger's mouth like the surf upon the beach, piling over one another in an ever-onward incessant assault upon the listener. Trailing behind him was a small retinue, striding vailantly to keep up.

"Set the canon there by that tree line!" Ottinger's command boomed like canon fire itself.

"It's our honor to have you perform this demonstration, sir," said Joshua James, even he, struggling to keep up with this force of nature. "To have the very man who has developed this remarkable device give us a personal demonstration…"

Ottinger continued as if James hadn't uttered a word. "From my work in the Ordnance Department, it's clear that the force required to project the ball via the cannonade is too great to consistently reach beyond 300 yards. Yet where do most wrecks occur? That's right, within 300 yards of shore."

"Oh, the Manby mortar is all well and good - within *one hundred* yards - but to shoot the projectile any further than that, well, it requires more black powder. More powder - greater explosive force. Greater explosive force, and no line cannot withstand that force, what with the projectile whizzing out and away. The line parts, and, basically, you're now firing a cannon ball at a sinking ship."

Captain Douglas Ottinger

Ottinger maintained a meticulously coiffed mustache that puffed out over his upper lip like that of a white walrus. It then worked its way under his chin, and strutted back toward his ears where it connected with some bushy sideburns. The whole assemblage gave him a steely touch of dash, and, despite its extravagance, actually seemed well-groomed.

"But the rocket, aye, the rocket, *this*, in my early years, seemed to be the answer. The problem with rockets, of course, is the direction. They are remarkably inconsistent although, I daresay, they've saved more than their share of lives in Europe."

"Set the cross-tree at my order. Count off, Lieutenant!" And with that Ottinger began to march off the yardage from the canon to the target. Ottinger was 6-3, big enough to be sure, but his energy made him seem enormous, stretching his booted feet forward in an exaggerated manner.

"Every man has a different gait, but every man can train himself to step forward precisely one yard, which is enormously useful in many lines of work, mine included."

"125, 126, 127..."

It was remarkable, but to look at him, it *did* seem as if every step was a precise replica of the one before it.

"It won't be long now, ladies and gentlemen," Ottinger announced to the small crowd that had gathered in the dune grass to watch the demonstration. Word had spread fast of Ottinger's arrival, and the demonstration of his new canon.

"151, 152, 153..."

"This is a new weapon against the senseless waste of lives on our shores." The man now seemed less like a tactician, and more like an impresario. He spoke as he marched off the distance. "Some 50 years ago, the frigate *Anson*, went upon the rocks near Land's End, England. The surf quickly beat this ship to pieces. A crowd gathered on the shore, and watched powerless as a crew of one hundred men perished. And only a few hundred yards from shore!"

"172, 173, 174..."

"Henry Trengrouse, a cabinetmaker from Heston Cornwall, was among that horrifed crowd, and he determined to do something about it. He sought to create a lightweight means of propelling a line to a ship."

"195, 196..."

"His chosen means for doing so was the rocket. His pioneering effort has lead us to this day, on this shoreline. No longer will people stand by helpless as fellow human beings suffer the cruel fate of the elements."

"222, 223..."

"Ottinger's Canon," he said, referring to himself as if he were something apart from himself, "will help us to win the war of the seas, right by our shores. A war to save lives, not waste them; a war to preserve the peace, not destroy it."

"249, 250."

Ottinger stopped and turned to the crowd for effect, standing as strong and lean as a telegraph pole.

"And you are here to witness this remarkable demonstration."

The crowd erupted in cheers with Cassandra and Dahlia clapping along. Ottinger's performace was remarkable by any standard, all the more so because it took place in the middle of a beach strafed bare by sun and wind, a cauldron of radiant light.

Dahlia caught Abraham Century's eye, and shot a little wave with her hand. Century turned away to his work without acknowledgement.Ottinger stepped back with a flourish, and nodded toward James.

"Men, erect the drill pole here!" James ordered.

Following a well-rehearsed series of actions, four of the men soon raised a 25-foot pole fixed with an eight-foot cross-spar on the exact spot of Ottinger's 250th step. When erect, this served nicely as the target mast for the drill. Then they rolled Ottinger's gun into position, the large creaky wheels lumbering over the uneven sand. Trask noticed Cassandra in the crowd.

"You've got five minutes, men. *Five* minutes." James reminded them.

To say that James had a reputation for punctuality would miss the target by a wide mark. He had already dismissed Barker from the service for slowing down a drill. (Barker was later re-admitted after visiting James seven days after the event, and pleading with him to take him back.) In this regard, James was the most remarkable of men in that he had an ironclad sense of time. He could awaken at any time during the morning, give or take 15 minutes, simply by willing himself to do so the night before. He had learned this, he said, during his 12 years on board ship, where one's watch could be changed daily, if the captain's whim required it.

"Take aim," James ordered. Trask and Murphy raised the gun, till Slocum said "Ho."

"Prepare to light the fuse," James said.

"Light the fuse."

Cassandra covered her ears as the flame kicked to life, twitching a twisted path along the fuse into the cannon. The cannon kicked back, and a plume of blue-white smoke issued forth into the air. The line whizzed sharply as it traced a wobbly arc across the lower sky.

The shot pulling the line fell short of the mark by a good 40 yards. Everyone looked at Ottinger who stared quizzically at the result for just a moment. He blinked once or twice.

"A heavier charge," he said softly to no one in particular. Then, to the crowd he barked. "A heavier charge is what's needed, that's all. A bit more of the *boom - boom*." And a big grin broke upon his face. "*Boom - boom*. More *boom - boom!*"

Everyone laughed, this being the very last reaction the crowd ever expected from the man.

Chapter Forty-Two

Three-Finger Riley

The sparks rise from the fire into the night like fragile souls leaving their hosts. Each burnt wisp, an orange faerie, rises up with the heated air...until the dark chill washes over it like a wave, extinguishing it - a vulnerable sprig swallowed...And the light, once raging with heat, is gone.

"We're all going to die, Gilbert," Thomas Mannering began, out of nowhere.

The driftwood seethed and hissed, interrupted by startling little pops. The heat is so intense now, it warps the air around it, creating strange distortions in the faces of the men as they look up across to one another.

The face of Jimmy Gilbert, round and rosy, looks as if it's underwater. Eyes unblinking like a dead man, he stares into the base of the fire mesmerized by the kaleidoscope of changing colors. Gilbert is determined not to encourage this line of thought.

"I mean, the drills, the equipment, the money, what's it all for, really?" Mannering pushed on. "What's the point of risking ourselves to save these people, most of whom you wouldn't even tip your hat to on the street."

A loud *pop* comes out of the fire, punctuating his statement. Gilbert continues to stare.

"I think it's just to pat ourselves on the rear end, that's all. Make us all feel a little less guilty for treating each other like bloody hell all the time. So we can wear our fancy coat on Sundays just like the rest of the bloodthirsty lunatics we share this town with."

"What's 'a matter with you, Mannering?" Gilbert couldn't stand it anymore. "You're a pup. What do you know about lifesaving? You couldn't save your breat' if I asked you to, which I am. Save your breat'."

The yellow and orange light from the fire reached out beyond the station house, illuminating the dunes. The wind whistled low and strange over through the spiky grass, and kicked up a brisk pelting of sand.

Mannering takes another slug from his flask.

"Don't breathe too close to the flames, ya' lush, your mouth'll catch fire," Gilbert hissed.

But Mannering forged on, emboldened by gin.

"I guess there's no mystery to it," Mannering continued after a pause. "I became a surfm'n because my father was a surfm'n, in his way. Worked the day all summer, looked out for people on the beach during the winter."

Gilbert flashed his wickedest scowl across the flames.

" 'Course they didn't do it for the money back then," Mannering straightened his shoulders. "All volunteer. My father saved 12 men, three of them were darkies."

"I know, they were all bloody saints," Gilbert starts up. "What you're not telling is all the loot this band of angels racked up on this very beach. They were little better than pirates. And Ol' Jeremiah Smith, he was the king of 'em all. Had the biggest house in town, and never worked an honest day in his life. How do you suppose he swung tha' one? By *caring fer the poor*?"

The virulence of Gilbert's speech stunned Mannering. Whereas before, he felt flush with the warmth of the gin and the fire's radiance, now he felt sickened. He took another slug, hoping it would cure it, and felt immediately worse.

"Wake up, Mannering. They did it for the same reasons we're out here freezing our nuts off - to make money, to keep our saggin' bags of flesh alive for another day. Only *they* were better at it. *They* hustled their way into houses and horse farms, wine from France, and whores in their pants. *Us?* We're pecking away at a government salary with no pension, and James, that old stone, tied 'round our necks."

Gilbert caught himself, and abruptly stopped. The sounds of this night on the beach suddenly rushed in and around the two men like a wave wrapping itself around some driftwood on the waterline. It surrounded them completely, lifted them up for a moment, and then laid them back down on the sand. The weather clearly wasn't getting any better.

"My god, call the local papers," Gilbert said, trying to put a bullet in the head of this conversation. "Mannering's got a bloody story to tell."

Just then, the edge of the sea lunged for the shore, gathered itself, and lunged again. Mannering's attention wandered to it for a moment as the insistent sound of it filled the empty space between him and Gilbert.

The bad gin and the bleakness of existence momentarily overwhelmed Mannering, like a child who has wandered in over his head, and is now completely engulfed in an angry wave.

"Hey Mannering," said the voice belonging to Jimmy Gilbert, "not to change the subject or anything, but has anyone told you the story of Three-Finger Riley?"

Mannering, startled from his revelry, turned to face the sound. Gilbert's face, lit by the dancing fire, seemed demonic. Gilbert was from County Cork in Ireland. He was mean when he was drunk; downright sadistic when he wasn't. Mannering, being English, was an early and often target of Gilbert's venom.

"Can't say they have."

"I'm surprised at the people around here, slacking off like that. A man going off on his first beach patrol, and not being told about Ol' Riley."

Gilbert straddled a log set across the fire from Mannering, and launched right into it. The freezing rain, now rather steady, zapped to steam in a quick *Zzzzt* as it hit the fire.

"Surfman Heinz, walking his patrol one night, came across

the body of a sailor named Riley who had been frozen in the ice along the shoreline.

"All that showed was a hand, appearing out of the ice from the wrist like a man reaching up from Death, trying to claw his way back to the land of the living."

Gilbert looked sideways at Mannering, trying to gauge the effect this drama was having on his audience.

"Underneath the ice, you could see Riley's face, frozen blue, with his eyes and mouth wide open looking up at Heinz...as if pleading with him to free him from the death panic in which he was frozen.

"Using his ax to get Riley out of the ice, the surfm'n accidentally chopped off two of Riley's fingers.

"Because of this, the ghost of Tom Riley would haunt poor Heinz on every patrol he took from that day on until one night, his fellow surfm'n found Heinz dead, frozen in the ice with two of *his* fingers cut off."

The fire hissed and popped at that moment for effect. Gilbert looked hard at Mannering's face. Then he leaned across the fire, his face distorted by the heated air rising before him, the freezing rain pelting his black rubber cap.

"There are people in this station house, Slocum for one, who say they sometimes hear Tom Riley's feet trudging behind them as they walk along this very beach in the darkness searching for his missing fingers."

Gilbert rolled up his sleeve, and arched three bony fingers into the night.

"Sometimes Ol' Riley will reach out his bloody stump of a hand," as he extended his cramped paw toward Mannering, "and GRAB YOU ON THE SHOULDER!!"

At that moment a hand grabbed Mannering's shoulder from behind.

"AAaaiiiii!" Mannering screamed as he jumped up off the log where he had been squatting.

Gilbert laughed so hard, it seemed as if his face would fall apart. As deep and primeval had been Mannering's scream, so too was the laughter of Gilbert...and his co-conspirator in the prank, Elijah Slocum, who had crept up behind the unsuspecting rookie, and grabbed him on cue.

It was the laughter of Zeus at the folly of Man, and it transformed the bleakness of this night on the beach into a carnival of delight. Even the insistent pounding of the waves upon the sand seemed more like tremendous peals of laughter breaking grin upon grin upon the otherwise green-grim sea.

"Did you see his face?!" Gilbert managed to blurt out among his paroxysms of glee.

Mannering, now slightly recovered, laughed along weakly.

"Thomas, trouble y'rslf, n' langer. 'Ere comes Barker. Back with the bloody coin. Y'll be making that long walk y'rslf, now." There was actually a touch of tenderness in Gilbert's voice, though it passed quickly.

"Barker! Trip over any bodies, man?"

"Yours would be the first, Gilbert."

"Aye, then make sure you take care of it. And don't go feeling it up and down before you give it back to the sea. There's nothing on me y'll ever want, I assure you."

Barker walked past the fire, and through the wooden doors of the station house.

Inside two men were playing checkers on the kitchen table, Jeremiah Slocum and Abraham Century. The light from a wobbly flame lit the center of the space, but did not reach the outer recesses of the room.

Barker walked to the cabinet where the log was kept, and made the following entry.

> 22:00 hours. Surfman Barker returned to station house. Wind: 12 knots SE, stiffening. Temperature: 25 degrees. Sea: choppy. Exchanged check with surfman Blacker of the Point O' Woods station at 20:00 hrs. No incidents on beach. No debris from shipwrecks. Passed check to Surfman Mannering at Lone Hill station. Mannering set out to the east immediately.

Mannering followed in behind Barker to don his gear.

"My brother says there's no such thing as bad weather, just bad clothing," Mannering ventured to break the silence.

"I've seen bad weather," Barker said without looking up from the log. "And I've worn good clothing...I think bad weather wins."

Barker flipped the coin across the room. Mannering surprised himself with a quick snag of it out of the air.

"You're it," Barker said as he headed up the ladder into the loft.

Mannering was already warmly dressed in three thick layers of wool. Now he wriggled his way into the outer layer, the oilskins - coarse, black rubber outerwear that was the surfmen's best defense against the elements.

He strapped on the rubber head gear, marked across the band with the insignia, FILILSS. The strap holding the Coston signal went over his shoulder, suspending the device, like the sheath of a general's sword, against his right side just above the belt. The Coston signals were flares that could be fired into the night sky to let the captain of a sea-going vessel that he was approaching dangerously close to shore. They were also used to let those whose ship had already run aground that they had been spotted. He stuffed some matches into his pocket, grabbed the spyglass and, of course, the coin, which he would hand to the watchman patrolling the beach from the east. Lastly Mannering picked up the oil lantern, filled with whale oil, and cautiously touched the wick with a lit match.

With that, Thomas Mannering walked out the door into the darkness alone. He paused for a moment by the bonfire, withdrew his hands from their gloves, and held them by the fire's heat. He looked out at the ocean roaring not 100 feet from where he stood, and saw the gathering hellfire.

Somewhere out there a ship is coming, he thought...

Soon to be broken by the blind sea, now silently it glides over the dark lair of an unseen monster. Insidious as an undertow, relentless as the tide, silent as the overarching moon, dark as this night, and patient, as if it understood Time, as if this fearsome clutch stretched from the very depth of Time itself, as if this monstrous presence WAS Time...

Thinking thus, his hands warmed, Mannering trudged off away from the fire, and down the dismal beach.

"I say, Mannering," Gilbert shouted out from somewhere, "watch out for Ol' Three-Finger Riley. Ha, ha, ha, ha..."

Chapter Forty-Three

On the Beach

Flecks of sand blister down the beach, and alight, randomly, it appears, yet, with what artful skill they are placed, carved into sinewy ribs, twisting like taut snakes on the beach.
Underwater the sand bottom is rippled just like that, by the current. Water, wind.
Smooth sea pebbles churn like a clean rugged emulsion under the waves - pulverizing, purifying - the sound of them grinding like the maw of some relentless beast. No large stones have resisted this dogged force, and the small ones are pounded ever smaller, to sand even. Little flecks of stone, blown apart, now blown around, in the hands of the wind of the air, the wind of the water.
But in whose hands the wind?

    In the Northeast United States, weather generally comes from the West. It gets pushed across the country by the stout command of the jet stream, traveling over the Rockies, across the plains westward, and busting out over the Atlantic Ocean.
    This pattern is fairly predictable, but there are some anomalies. During the winter months, from November to February, some storm systems called Nor'east'rs surge northward up the coastline. A Nor'east'r gets its name from the relentlessly powerful northeasterly winds that blow in from the ocean ahead of the storm, i.e., the winds blow in the direction of the Northeast.
    Nor'east'rs are among the most ferocious of storms here.

A single nor'east'r can move more sand on or off a barrier beach than decades of regular wave-driven erosion. New inlets can appear overnight. Navigational maps are immediately rendered useless. The bottom features a wholly new contour. Beach dunes become sea bottom.

If the nor'east'r travels up the eastern coastline just out over the Atlantic the moisture coming up off the sea is sucked into the gathering vortex. The sea is transfigured by the impending storm into a raw power supply, fueling this locomotive like coal in a boiler.

Thus, properly formed and fueled, and headed on destiny's pitched path, nor'east'rs of this type careen brutishly northward up the coast, whipping waves into oversized agents of their arrival, and smothering the coastline with a wicked white discharge.

On this night, as Thomas Mannering began his watchful walk down the beach just such a storm was bearing northward toward the barrier beach Fire Island. But, for now, the wind slept - a killer cat in repose. Soon, it would rise, arch its back, and tread confidently in search of its prey.

The first indicator of this monster was a rustle, a brief poof, the merest force, a laughingstock, a caricature of wind itself. But in short order, it gathered in intensity, rising to a respectable blow.

Wind is air in motion. But from where comes the force that drives the air that whips itself around every object bold enough to stand? What is the force *behind* the force that sheers through the dune grass, peppering sand against driftwood, and pushing trees back, till they give up their leaves, till they are straining the conviction of their very roots, making a mockery of their claim to permanence. Limbs tear away, and hang from their trunks sadly. Some topple over into the sand and dirt, their useful life spent, soon to be food for bugs.

At times, this force lies quiet; at others, it rouses itself with epic propensity, creating an unholy commotion over the land and sea, a howling, like the rage of God.

Even before the rain comes, the water coming off the wavetops is blown across the beach, so that it feels like rain. When the temperature is near freezing, as it was on this first night of the storm, the conditions are at their worst. The spray, blown by the bitter wind, crystallizes to ice almost before it hits the sand.

The top 1/4 inch of sand on the beach is entirely crystallized with a thin glaze of crackling ice from this phenomenon, ice so brittle that each of Thomas Mannering's footfalls rang out with a sound like the blunt crushing of brittle glass bells, as his boots stumped and bluffed through the hoary casement of thin craggy ice that clung to the frosty sand. The moisture was everywhere.

Mannering leaned into the fresh force of this new wind. The light from his lantern swayed and gyrated in accordance with his gait, fitfully illuminating a 25-foot diameter circle around him.

Something in the surf attracts Mannering's eye - a wine bottle. Holding it up to the lantern, he sees that inside the bottle is a handwritten note. He takes off his gloves, and carefully retrieves it from the bottle.

The gusting wind makes reading the note a difficult task so Mannering flattens it on the sand, and brings the lamp closer. There, on all fours, past midnight on the beach beneath the night sky, Thomas Mannering reads these words:

> *February 8th, 1853 6 p.m., on board the Louise V. Place. She has foundered upon a sandbar, is at mercy of the seas, half-full of water. God help us. Captain Squires is already washed overboard.*
> *Charles Allen, Engineer*
Providence, Rhode Island

Just then, the wind lifted a corner of the note off the sand, revealing writing on the other side as well.

> *The finder of this note will please communicate with my wife, and let her know of my death.*

Mannering tries to imagine this man, freezing to death on the deck of the foundering vessel with the presence of mind to write this note, find a bottle, cork it, and send it off upon the waves that were about to engulf him.

Fire Island...the refuse of the relentless power of the ocean, an afterthought of storms...immense tonnage of sand, carried grain by grain...hidden handiwork beneath the vast plains of undulating, pummeling gray-green, blue black water. Alone upon that restless churning, a man's final act - hoping in the very absence of hope, to reach someone, even after the waves has long since devoured him...

"Hallow! Hallow!"

Mannering hears the hailing from down the beach. It is his counterpart from the Blue Point station patrolling the beach toward him. It startles him from his reverie, and, in an inexplicable way, makes him feel ashamed that he had been indulging in such thoughts. He feels inside-out, exposed to his fellow man.

"Hallow!"

"Hallow! Mannering here!"

"Thomas Swanson. You the new man?"

"I am."

"Have a smoke?"

"Delighted."

"C'mon, the fire's already lit."

Swanson and Mannering walk up the beach away from the surf into the brambles, beach roses and dune grass that pass for vegetation in this windswept terrain. There, Mannering follows Swanson to a tiny six-by-ten foot room, a half-way house.

Into these confines Mannering from the new Lone Hill lifesaving station passed with Swanson from the Blue Point lifesaving station, a man he had never met before...

A monk's solitary retreat would be better equipped. Two

rickety chairs filled the space with a fireplace, driftwood and matches. But Mannering was grateful for the fire, and the company.

"Bring an extra pipe for just such occasions."

Mannering could hardly speak for the joy he felt as he watched Thomas Swanson fill two pipes with the dry leafy tobacco that he had pulled from somewhere beneath his oilskins.

"Wicked night tonight," was all Swanson said just before he lit the first pipe, and handed it to Mannering.

"Virginia's finest, right there. You can't find any better."

Swanson's hospitality enveloped Mannering like a soft ocean wave in August. After his two-hour patrol alone in the darkness, and his bleak ponderings, the fellowship was almost more than his heart could bear.

"I found this note in a bottle," Mannering ventured.

"That's a find."

"It's from a Mr. Charles Allen from the *Louis V. Place*."

"The *Place*! I was a part of that rescue. Everyone froze in the rigging. It was ghastly duty, bringing those bodies down in the storm."

"What happened?"

Swanson took a long snatch from his pipe before answering. The glowing red embers momentarily illuminated his intense gaze. He exhaled a plume of white smoke which tarried for a moment, then disappeared. The sound of the roiling waves - agitated, restless, seething - swelled into the sudden quiet space between the two men. Mannering could now see what a dashing figure Swanson was.

"The night of the wreck was the worst storm in several decades," Swanson began. "The temperature was dead zero. The winds were clocked at 68 miles an hour at Block Island. They had been beating to the north-northeast for days, then shifted westward causing a furious cross-sea.

"By the morning of the 8th, the *Louis V. Place*, a three-masted schooner, ran up on a bar where the surf proceeded to pound her to pieces. The surf was like slushy oatmeal thick with ice some two-feet deep, and some of the breakers were a good 20-feet tall. There were cakes of ice piled six-foot high on the beach.

"Launching a boat in those conditions was not possible," he said dryly.

The reflections from the fire illuminated Swanson's face in an ominous manner. He took another pull from his pipe, and continued.

"The vessel couldn't have been more than 400 yards from the beach, but we couldn't see it for the darkness and the gale. We knew some of the crew were still alive though. We could hear their wailing, or thought we could, through the howling of the storm.

"By the time daylight arrived there were only two people left alive in the rigging. There was one other, but he swung from the ratlines like a skinned chicken.

"It wasn't until midnight on Saturday, 40 hours after the vessel went aground, that we were able to launch the boat."

Swanson stopped talking, and looked dolefully into the fire.

After a long pause, he started up again. "Funny: each of us walking around, strangers to one another, islands unto ourselves, the same flame burning hot inside us all, though - like an island of fire. A fire island is what we are. Someone I think named this beach just about right - Fire Island."

Mannering looked down at the note in his hands.

"Allen asks that the finder of the note tell his wife about his death," he said.

"Then you shall do it."

The directness of the command stunned Mannering. Swanson abruptly stood up from his perch.

"You'll be needing this," Swanson said, and handed Mannering his coin, marked with the insignia of the United States Lifesaving Service, Blue Point Station.

Mannering, in turn, gave Swanson his coin.

This exchange of coins was evidence to the station keepers that both men had indeed performed their patrol, and met each other on the beach. If a patrolmen didn't come back with the coin, and the keeper asked for it, he could be asked to re-walk the patrol.

It was a simple act, yet, upon receiving the coin, Mannering felt as though a mighty gong had been struck within him. His body and soul rung with its vibration, and filled him with a sense of the holy. As he watched Swanson kicking sand to extinguish the fire, Mannering fingered the coin in his pocket, rubbing it like a talisman, as if it were something sacred that was his solemn duty to safely transport back to the world of men.

"Take care, Mannering," Swanson said just outside the door, "you wouldn't want the Ol' Man to start worrying about you."

With that, he turned on the soles of his feet, and bounced away into the darkness. It would have been unseemly to look after him for any more than a moment, though that is exactly what Mannering wanted to do. Instead, Mannering trudged off down the beach to where he felt it was safe, then turned around to look.

Swanson was gone, of course - the smell of his tobacco, like the puff of smoke that carried it, gone; that bristling athletic energy leaping off his figure like an Olympian, gone; his presence already a memory. The space which he once occupied was now completely re-filled by the darkness.

The thought occurred to Mannering that he might never see Swanson again. This one brief encounter may have been it for a lifetime.

All at once, the walk back to the station house loomed before him. It seemed interminable - just sand, sea, darkness, and, worse, the black thoughts that filled his head like a pool of water left on the shore long after the tide has retreated.

FIRE ISLAND

"Take care, Mannering..."

Chapter Forty-Four

Wailing in the Wind

Thomas Mannering trudged back toward the lifesaving station as if he were walking through another world. The warm glow of his meeting with Swanson was now gone. The cold wind had stripped his body and mind clean to where he felt as gaunt and lean as a skeleton. The tide has risen, considerably, since the patrol out, and had swallowed up the impressions his boots had made in the frosty sand. Just keep walking, he told himself. Just keep walking.

Little was left of his well-being at this moment, but a simmering fire in the core of his being, and a determination to get back to the warmth of the station house. The wind was blowing steady now, 55-60 knots with gusts up to 80. So strong it was, that a real force of effort was required to make progress into it, by foot, never mind by boat. It was a Nor'east'r, all right, a real stinger.

Occasionally, he would stop, and scan out to sea, but what he saw there only encouraged him to walk faster. It was a wicked tumult, an indiscernible tumble of waves, wind, rain and darkness accompanied by the unrelenting roar of the ocean pounding the beach.

At one point, he thought he saw the dark profile of a vessel. But the storm immediately closed around it. He had been told about the "ghostly outlines of vessels long-lost" that would deceive a surfman's eyes as he strained to see real vessels in a storm. These mirages were conjured by an overactive mind, he was told, much like a wayfarer may see a longed-for lake in the midst of a barren desert. He was sternly told by his colleagues to confirm a sighting before lighting the alert flare, the Coston signal.

The Coston signal was the surfman's chief means of signaling that a wreck had been spotted. It served a dual function: one of letting the stranded sailors know they had been seen, and help was arriving, and two, of signaling the surfmen at the nearby station houses of the same. The Coston signal consisted of a wooden handle fixed on one end with a flare, and on the other with a spring-loaded plunger that, when hit with the heel of one's hand, would light the signal flare.

Mannering walked on, but the silhouette of the vessel haunted him. More than likely it was Swanson's story of the *Louis V. Place* replaying itself in his mind. But what if it *were* a ship? It seemed unlikely on his first patrol, but the conditions certainly justified his suspicion. He held the spyglass to his eye again, and cursed the rain splattering on the lens. There, *he saw it again*! This time, he even thought he heard the sound of sails luffing in the wind.

He stared hard into the storm, motionless like a Chesapeake Labrador pointing at fallen prey. His eyes peered through the rain, the darkness, even the icicles that had formed on his lashes. Was it an apparition? Without thinking now, he held the Coston signal away from his body, and banged the plunger. It ignited immediately, a fierce crimson deflagration, reddening the darkness.

Moments later he saw a distress flare from a vessel tear through the night sky like glowing red sword.

FIRE ISLAND

Chapter Forty-Five

Ship Ashore!

The crimson glare from the distant signal dawned upon the brow of Joshua James like a new morning. This was a man born with what was called "3 o'clock courage." He was one of those rare men who could be awakened in the middle of the night, and be ready for battle before he got his pants on.

His eyelids twitched open, the pupils dilated. His mind took an instant to focus.

Then, Gilbert, the watch, burst into his room.

"Mr. James, two flares down the beach."

"Wake the men. Ring the bell."

"This is not a drill, men," his voice boomed through the station house. "This is *not* a drill."

James donned his gear in methodical fashion, without emotion. He, along with his men, had practiced this very routine scores of times. He was the first man outfitted, and stood like a sentry at the entrance, looking in. Reflections from the fire blazing just outside the door flitted dully off the burnished black rubber of his oilskins. His oafish cap already strapped underneath his chin and pulled low over his eyes would have made him look silly if not for the staunch erectness of his posture. Even in complete stillness his slight body seemed full of power and life.

He did not shout orders. The men through hour upon hour of tedious drilling knew what to do.

Abraham Century and three men went out to the boathouse to

harness Gypsy to the boat carriage. Gilbert and his crew gathered the Lyle gun with the lines coiled in the fakir box. Slocum, the house cook, quickly gathered some food that would travel well. There was no telling how long they would be.

They were ready to travel in nine minutes.

Warmed by a fire's glow, safe within stout and familiar walls, they are too soon before the unclothed face of darkness. Courage - Will - are not the equal of this mighty beast, howling. It will splinter a man shorn of meaning like kindling blistering before an axe.

"Men!" Joshua James sang out into the wind. "*Ho!*"

Abraham Century slapped Gypsy's hind quarters, and she kicked into a steady pull. *Audacious* slowly exited the station house.

In dry conditions the lightness of the vessel made it relatively easy to transport over the yielding pliant sand. But the severity of this storm presented other difficulties. Gypsy, for one, had become spooked by the wall of noise that was issuing from the ocean. The sea was indeed mountainous. It created a steady continuous roar that eroded the confidence of the entire crew, no less a horse. She stopped time and again, and had to be coaxed forward by Abraham Century who knew her best. James commanded the men to push the cart from behind forcing the

"There're lives in the balance."

poor horse forward at the head of the carriage. She dug in her hooves, and began to bray, and kick up her heels. Nothing could calm the spooked animal.

"Century, release the horse!" James shouted. "We'll have to pull the cart ourselves."

After being released from the harness, Gypsy reared up on her hind legs, and snapped the lead out of Century's hand. She galloped away frantically down the beach back toward the station house enveloped quickly by the night which closed in behind her.

"Gypsy!" Century shouted, as he began to run after her.

"Century!" James commanded. "Return to the boat!"

Century's momentum carried him forward a bit, and then he caught himself up. Sheepishly, he turned around, embarrassed at his outbreak of emotion for the horse, now gone off into the darkness somewhere.

"She's not going anywhere," Gilbert growled. "She'll be warming her rump by the fire, like we all will soon."

The expression, coming though it did from the cynically curled lips of Jimmy Gilbert, sent a bolt of confidence through the entire crew.

"At least we've got Reef, men," Gilbert continued. "Reef's not going anywhere, are you, boy." The Newfoundland looked up at Gilbert with his sloppy brown doleful eyes. The dog, obviously expecting a long night with wet fur, gave a cursory wag of his tail, and plodded on, bonded inextricably to this crew on the beach.

"You men, at the head of the carriage, and pull," James commanded. "Barker, mind the wheels at the rear."

Just then Mannering emerged from the envelope of darkness on the beach, his chest heaving from a two-mile run down the beach. He was apoplectic, gasping for breath, and barely able to speak.

" 'S'a wreck, sir," he managed to say between paroxysms. "Debris - on the beach."

Another red flare from the ship pierced the night sky. It's powerful though short-lived burst of colored light illuminated each of the faces that looked upward. For an instant, the beach was transformed by a ghastly reddish illumination. But the storm made quick work of these feeble pyrotechnics, extinguishing it like a lit match tossed overboard.

"Forward men," James voice piped up just before the light faded. "There're lives in the balance."

Chapter Forty-Six

Men in the Rigging

Trask felt his insides threshing about, like a fish thrust suddenly on land. He thought for sure he would vomit on the beach from the excitement.

He looked toward the place where the flares had been. Within that darkness hid an encounter with something dimly remembered, a remote dream, unraveling in reverse, *deja vu*, through a dark mirror. He had that queer feeling again, like he had during his walk with Grinnell, of being a ghost peering in on his old life, but from a different angle: with *one* leg this time - from the beach, not the boat - as the savior, not the saved.

For a moment, this feeling became so real, he fully expected to find Josh on the foundering vessel. In spite of the irrationality of the impression, the chance of saving his son blossomed again, like a bud that blooms from within itself, over and over again, continuously opening out in a never-ending series of hopeful extensions into time and space.

So enthralling was this revelry, that it obliterated any normal sensations - of cold, fatigue, or fear. He glanced sideways at the other men, careful that they not notice him looking at them. How distant they seemed! How alone here on the beach!

Then, he looked at Joshua James strutting like a penguin, his chest thrust forward, chin extended, eyes forward, neck holding his head upright and steady. Nothing seemed to deter him - not the roar of the surf, the pelting of the sand, nor the bite of the salty ice crystals whipping off the wavetops.

Swept up in his revelry, Trask understood James for the first time. This man spent *all* of his time in that uplifted firmament of Courage, Fortitude, Compassion and Heroism. He suffered not the opprobrium other men sought to cast upon him - talking, as some were wont, behind his back, ridiculing his silly quirks. He was doing battle on a higher plain. He was wrestling with demigods that most men couldn't even see. There, for James, resided Victory and Defeat.

And then, as Trask pondered the wonders of the man, James spoke as if on cue.

"The principle danger in effecting this rescue will be from the heavy sea running," he said.

It was a simple statement of fact, but it seemed to settle the men, who were grinding out the yards behind him rolling the cart over the rain-softened sand. At spots, the beach was flooded as far as the sand dunes with water sluicing through tidal gulleys impeding their progress. Each of these tidal rivers were fordable, fortunately, though with each passing the men's labors intensified.

"It is my opinion that no other boat, except the one we have, can get alongside this vessel in these conditions," James said to no one in particular. "No boat that I know of."

As the surfmen approached the position of the wreck, they could hear the weak cries of its crew in the dark. It quickened their hearts to hear them, woefully moaning into the maelstrom, though the vessel still could not be seen.

"Barker, position the Lyle gun here. Slocum, send up a flare."

The men hopped to their work in a darkness most complete. The lanterns, covered in sleet, eked out a feeble light. And the moon, lost high above the dense and menacing clouds of this muscular storm, cast a hopeless radiance that would never reach those below.

Great blocks of ice cakes, 4-6 feet tall, towered on the shore with portentous aspect like the ominous visage of tribal statues. Wreckage from the doomed ship littered the beach.

After several attempts, Slocum ignited the flare, sending its red comet of light into the teeth of the wind. *There it was*! The vessel, not 300 yards from shore! The sight of it stunned the crew for a moment, much like the impact the first sighting of a whale has upon the crew of a whale ship that has prepared for its encounter for a long time.

Three of the men lifted the brass Lyle gun out of the cart, a hefty 165 pounds. An oak carriage cradled the small canon, clasps of iron bound it in place. Two men followed behind the canon with the "faking" box, a wooden box studded with 4-inch wooden pegs inside. During their long hours of preparation for rescue, the men had carefully coiled the shot line upon the pegs.

The men overturned the box, setting the meticulously coiled architecture of rope upon the frosty beach sand. They had stitched the rope fastidiously so that when the projectile is fired at the ship, the line will uncoil without a hitch. An eyebolt, secured to the top of the six-pound lead missile, carries the fastened shotline to the stranded vessel.

The eyebolt is all that remained visible of the projectile as it sat in the muzzle of the gun waiting to be fired at the target.

The Lyle Gun

James preferred using a number-9 line as the shotline because lighter lines tended to break. But once a shotline gets wet, as it will in this weather, any gauge line was likely to part upon firing.

"Ignition ready!" James shouted into the wind. "At my command, carry the canon forward. Plant, aim and fire."

As they had so often done during their drills, James waited for a slatch tide, a short period of smooth surf, before commencing the canon firing sequence. After the final wave before the onset of a slatch tide had spent its tonnage upon the beach, James will order the men carrying the canon to follow the receding wave back into the ocean - and closer to the stranded vessel. Working quickly, the men will lower the canon into the newly-revealed sand, choose an elevation setting on the notched wooden block at the rear of the canon, and light the fuse. The shot is fired, and, if all goes well, the projectile will reach its mark before the next wave returns to the beach.

Yet, despite the months of training in this drill, the men knew how slim were the odds of success. Predicting a slatch tide, for example, was a bit of hocus-pocus at best, even for a man as familiar with this beach as Joshua James. Lighting a match, and putting it to the fuse under these circumstances was a crap shoot. A flare had to be successfully launched just prior to the tidal rush, otherwise the men could not see the vessel, the hoped-for target of their aim.

The men stood at the ready while James peered into the surf, seeking the inscrutable rhythm of the waves. One slatch tide clearly passed; James had missed it. Then another. Still, the men stood motionless in the gale.

"Ready men."

"Slocum, light the flare."

The red fire ball arced bravely into the vague gray wetness.

"We'll follow this next wave back. Forward, men!"

Four men raced forward carrying the canon between them. Slocum followed alongside with the matches tucked underneath his oilskins.

"Now, down!..Set your aim!..Ignite the fuse!"

After two wet and wobbly attempts, Slocum tossed the first sorry match, unlit, into the wet sand. He quickly fumbled for a second match, and dragged its head smartly across the abrasive surface on the side of the matchbox. *Ignition.*

Slocum cupped his hand around the upstart flame carefully shielding it from the everywhere wet wind. He carefully guided the flame toward the fuse as the sea gathered itself for its next big push up the beach slope. At first, no sparks flew when flame and fuse were brought together. Then, the fuse sputtered, but, being damp, quickly lost its drive toward ignition. Slocum persisted, and with the match flame faltering to extinction, the fuse finally jumped to life. Sputtering fitfully at first, it built upon itself, and pulled its way, seemingly fist over fist, up the dangling line of the fuse.

Just before the fuse flame disappeared into the back end of the canon, the storm swallowed Slocum's flare. The world waited then, for an eternity in an instant, for the explosion that never happened.

"Bring in the canon men!"

James' voice from the beach brought the men back to their senses. And not a moment too soon. As they hustled up the sandy slope, a wave crashed around their ankles. The churning water rose up to mid-thigh, forcing the men to raise the 165 pound canon up over their heads.

"Check the powder," James ordered.

His suspicions were well-founded for, upon inspection, the entire canister of powder was found to be wet beyond use. Eck and his men had gotten to it, though James couldn't know this at the time. What he did know was that all the air had just gone out of the sails of their first rescue attempt.

"Slocum. Gilbert. Return to the station, and retrieve some dry powder. Be quick about it," he called after them.

The two men jogged off back down the beach, with Reef trotting alongside them. The remaining crew jangled their circulatory systems with little jumps, and clapped their gloved hands together instinctively. The extremities had already succumbed to the brute facts of this night. And the relentless march of the cold wet darkness was working its way inexorably toward the heated core of each man.

Chapter Forty-Seven

Eck

"There's no dry powder where they're going," said Frank Eck as he took the spyglass away from his eye. "Is there, Joe?"

Joe the Indian looked up from under his hands shielding his eyes from the rain. "Dry? No. Most definitely not dry. A lot wet though."

"Hah!" Eck cackled once. "You're a good man, Joe. And good men are always rewarded. Says so in the good book, doesn't it, my good friend."

Supercargo Butler stared into the rain, disconsolate. "How long are we going to be out here, Eck?"

"Could be worse, my friend. You could be back cleaning stalls for Ol' Man Murphy, where I found you. Remember that? Saluting that old fool every morning with a happy 'how are you' when all you really wanted to do was drop a bucket of slop over his head. Let's not forget where we all came from."

He brought the spyglass to his eye again. "And where we're all going."

"I can't even feel my hands."

Eck looked down at Butler with a sneer, and lifted the spyglass to his eye once more.

"They're moving again boys, down the beach...That ship is adrift...I think they're in for a long night, heh, heh - a *real* long night."

Chapter Forty-Eight

Darkness

What Eck had failed to consider, however, was the blind persistence of Joshua James.

"Fire!"

The canon blasted the rope-carrying projectile into complete darkness. The concussion stunned the men for a moment, as the shotline whipped out of the faking box, whistling sharply as it did.

The line seemed to be riding up and off the surf as if it were being suspended on the far end by the spars of the vessel. A good sign.

"Slocum, light another flare," James commanded.

When the red fireball soared into the air, the men cheered. Finally, a direct hit! The shotline arced from the rigging perfectly, as if it had been placed there by some magic. Even James allowed himself a moment of exultation.

And, by the light of the flare, he could see, if only faintly, the figure of a man beginning the climb up the foremast to secure the line to the vessel.

"BRING IN THE LINE!" James shouted to the vessel, though it was unlikely that anyone could hear him in the gale. The flare failed quickly, dropping the black velvet night curtain over the vessel once again.

The men erected the ten-foot wooden cross they had brought with them from the station house. The cross consisted of two pieces of 2 x 3 inch hardwood bolted together in the shape of an X. It was buried deep into the sand for stability. With the shotline run through the crotch of the X, the cross served to keep the line up and over the surf throughout its expanse from the beach to the rigging of the vessel.

"Bring in the line!"

But within minutes, the line drooped heavily with frozen rain and sea spray. At mid-distance, it sagged into the surf.

Slocum shot another flare into the gray storm.

James raised the spyglass to his eye. "I don't see him," he muttered out loud.

"Wait...there he is...in the cross spar...I believe he's got hold of the line..."

Just then, the taut line went slack. Somehow, it had come free from the vessel, perhaps it was the heaviness of the frozen line, or the numbness of the man's hands that couldn't hold it. In any case, the men pulled the line back to shore. Frozen as it was, this line could not be re-shot at the vessel so the men lifted another faking box filled with coiled rope out of the cart.

Several lines were fired across the vessel, but with each, the shot either missed its mark, or hit its mark, and quickly snapped like the thread of a seamstress.

The crew from the Blue Point Station had since joined those of the Lone Hill Station, but their arrival didn't change the status of the rescue. After each failed attempt, the surfmen hauled themselves further down the beach, anticipating the drift of the stranded vessel. James would declare another spot, and try again.

But, as the tide was rising, with each subsequent effort, the odds of success became slimmer. The men, once again, dug their way frantically through the frozen beach sand to plant the sturdy sand anchor for the hawser line. The last line was fired...and soon after, abandoned, somewhere among the cordage clotting the surfline.

"Strike the cross, and load everything back into the cart. We'll have to try the lifeboat." James knew that calling for the launch of the lifeboat put the lives of every surfman at risk.

The men hopped to his orders, but, like the darkness that kept washing over the brief burst of light from Slocum's flares, a pall enveloped the men's morale. The hope for a quick and safe rescue, unlikely in any case, now disappeared completely.

FIRE ISLAND

Chapter Forty-Nine

The Launch of the Life Boat

"Mr. Century," James commanded, "help us off, then stand-to on the beach."

Century was stunned by the command. He belonged in the boat. He was number one. It was because he couldn't swim, of course, and in these seas, *Audacious* would likely capsize at least once, if not several times before the crew would be able to launch her, if at all.

A man who couldn't swim would be a dangerous liability under those circumstances. Yet Century was angry and hurt nonetheless. Shame replaced cold as the predominant sensation in his body.

Listlessly, he donned his cork lifevest along with the other men. His vest though, was ridiculously undersized for his massive frame which only increased his sense of shame. The other men averted their eyes from his, as if they were conspirators in a caper, though, of course, it was James' call, and James' call alone.

"Heave to, men." The crew struggled with *Audacious*, lifting the boat off the cart, and on down the beach. The surf greeted them like a wall of fury. Morale bottomed out when faced with the imminent prospect of launching into the roiling porridge, peppered with an ominous tangle of ice and debris from the wreck.

James picked out a spot in the leeward "shadow" of the

stranded vessel, to take advantage of the slight break in the surf provided by the hulk. It seemed the height of folly to even think of launching a boat into this maelstrom, but James was not to be deterred. He proceeded as if unaware of the odds against him.

"Stand ready, men..."

Abraham Century stood at the stern of the boat, blinking back the frozen rain that pelted his face. He kept his face turned away from the wind, so he could hear James' commands. Jimmy Gilbert, Thomas Mannering and Skull Murphy, looking like pallbearers, manned the port side. On the starboard side were Elijah Slocum, John Barker and Trask, already up to their knees in it. James took his position next to Century at the rear.

"At my command..."

"*Now!*"

The men all pushed at once, and *Audacious* set off nicely. As they had so often during drills, they pulled themselves into the boat at James' command, and soon the boat was fully loaded.

The great challenge of such a launch was to get beyond the breakers as fast as possible. To do so meant keeping the bow headed dead straight into the surf, and having the men pull fast and hard. A little luck couldn't hurt either.

To hit these rollers at even the slightest of angles would spill the boat, dumping everyone ignominiously into the boil.

Not that they could be any wetter than they already were. The crew was incessantly drenched with the icy water coughed up high over the bow as the boat withstood one hammer blow after another from the incoming waves. It froze upon their oilskins as soon as it struck, and hardened to a bitter crackling mail.

James stood tall in the stern, leaning on the rudder. But, as the small boat pitched up and over a wave, the rudder would split the sea, and James would lose control of the steering. He had all he could do to keep the vessel headed into the surf. But, incredibly, the launch was successful in the first attempt.

Trask and the other men pulled and pulled at James' command. Had they ever doubted James' insistence on military discipline, they never would again. Without their focus on their duty, without obeying their commander, without working as a team, in a moment they would all be swallowed by the sea.

As it was, the little crew seemed puny in the midst of these mountainous swales. But, mercifully, concentrating on their efforts shielded their thoughts from the peril that surrounded them.

But as the *Audacious* approached the stricken vessel, Trask peered over his shoulder, and lost his nerve. The stranded vessel was a complete catastrophe. His rowing lost rhythm; his arms felt like lead and, worst of all, the image of Josh started flashing through his mind again.

"*Aargh*. I'm getting a bloody blister on my ass!" yelled Gilbert.

And more than one man commiserated. The wet oilskins rubbing against the hard wooden bench of the boat gave the rowers one more reason to wish they were home.

"Almost there, men," cautioned James. "Almost there."

"Look in the masts, sir!" yelled Mannering.

"*Port, row. Starboard, lay off.*"

Dark lumps broke the straight line of the mast silhouette as it cut its harsh swath across the charcoal sky. One of the figures seemed to be waving, though it was too dark to tell if it was an arm gesturing or one of the lines swaying in the gale.

"Port, row. Starboard, lay off," James commanded.

Audacious approached the battered hulk to leeward. James planned on coming between it and the beach, using the sullen vessel as a wind breaker. This strategy would make it easier to keep

Audacious close enough to the wreck to affect a rescue.

Had he chosen to come at the wreck from the windward side, the side of the wreck that faced out to sea, he would expose the crew to a considerable risk – that of having *Audacious* slammed into the grounded vessel upon approach.

Of course the leeward side had its risks as well. A tangled mess of debris dangled from the vessel to leeward like the tentacles of an ornery jellyfish – lines, wooden chucks of the wreck, spars and sails. The chop was littered like a frothy-gray soup.

"Together now. Pull! Pull!"

James cozied *Audacious* to within 25 feet of the boat. Now, 20 feet. Now 15. But there seemed to be no opening in the debris to allow for actual contact.

"Ciao!" someone shouted from on-board the vessel "*Sopra qui!*" The man was Italian! For the first time, Trask glanced at the name of the broken vessel - *Nuova Speranza*.

"*Ciao! Sopra qui!*"

"Standby. We're coming," James yelled in response.

But the desperate man kept up his call. Over and over again, he hailed the rescue vessel. "*Ciao! Sopra qui!*" "*Ciao! Sopra qui!*"

The debris in the water clogged the men's oars, making forward progress impossible. Again and again, James attempted an approach without success. At one point, he instructed his men to grab hold of one of the lines trailing from the vessel, and pull the boat in, but *Audacious* nearly capsized in the effort.

James reminded himself that the lives of his crewmembers were at risk, as well as those who still lived on-board the *Nuova Speranza*.

"*Ciao! Sopra qui!*"

"Godammit man! I can't stand it. Y're bleating like a sheep!"

Gilbert was standing in the boat now, yelling at the wreck.

"If y' don't shut-up, we'll leave y' here. Then y'll get quiet, 'n' stay quiet fer a long time…"

"Mr. Gilbert, compose yourself," James said.

"Do we have to save him?" Gilbert cracked, as he sat back down. "Sharks have to make a living too, y' know."

"Mr. Gilbert…"

"Who'd know? One quick kick, and he's shark food, and no one's the wiser, *eh*, boys?"

"*Ciao! Sopra qui!*"

"*Aargh…*" Gilbert moaned, and rolled his eyes. "He didn't understan' a single word I said."

The incoming waves had pushed the grounded vessel on her side. Leaning shoreward, her mainmast, the only mast left standing on the vessel, hovered directly over the *Audacious* on her closest approach. The situation spawned an idea in James' mind.

"We're going to attach a line to that mast, and board the vessel that way."

The crew exchanged a sideways glance.

"Mr. Slocum, at my command, toss that line over the cross-spars."

"Starboard…pull, pull. Together now. Pull! Pull!"

Slocum bounced the rope coil in his hand, nervously measuring the weight and resistance of it. He looked straight up at the gothic spire towering overhead. It was a toss of a good 25 feet from a rolling boat, into the teeth of a hurricane wind.

"Stand-by Mr. Slocum. Set your aim. Standby…Let her go…"

With a muscular grunt, Slocum uncorked a mighty heave, propelling the uncoiling rope into the dark sky beyond sight. And, like a magic rope conjured into the air by a magician, the extended rope suddenly pulled taut. It had found its target!

The crew exploded into a round of cheers with Slocum the hero.

John Barker grabbed the far end of the rope, now dangling in the water, and quickly tied a bowline knot. Slocum pulled down on his side of the line, and the bowline traveled up into the darkness toward the cross spar. When it arrived, Slocum pulled taut with his full body weight, and the bowline grabbed tight.

"That's not going anywhere," Slocum announced firmly.

"Trask." The sound of his name coming from Joshua James struck like a blow to his stomach.

"At my command, you're to climb aboard. Bring a line with

you. Make a foothold in it, and tie if off on that spar. You're to lower the survivors into the vessel."

There was no further explanation or discussion. James knew the peril to which he had just put Trask. Yet there was a clear-headed logic to choosing him. Since losing his leg, Trask had developed an abnormally strong upper body, especially his arms. He had made it something of a personal mission to build his strength. As his bunkmates could attest, he could do 200 military style push-ups at a clip. What's more, without a leg, the ratio of his upper body strength to the overall weight of his body was far greater than any other man on the boat. Trask was clearly the right choice for this mission.

Trask lashed a coil of rope to his waist, and, without a word of farewell, clasped the hanging line, and jumped off and away from *Audacious*.

He immediately began swaying and twisting in the wind. But soon, he got his bearings, and, hand over hand, raised himself up into the mast. As he did, he reminded himself sternly not to look down. The churning morass waiting to engulf all falling objects would have chilled the courage of any man.

He grabbed hold of the icy cross-spar with one hand, then two. He hoisted himself up, and slung his leg over the top of it. Down below the men cheered.

Trask lay on the spar for a moment, his chest heaving.

A strange sensation came over him…*Here he was again*! Face down on an icy spar of a floundering vessel just off shore in a hurricane. The odd thought occurred to him that he could have been almost anywhere at that moment – in front of the fire in Cassandra's living room, drinking rum in a saloon on Cherry Street…anywhere. But he was here, now, in great peril, 25 feet from his death. By choice…

Why, he wondered. *Why*?

He saw Josh again, not in his final moments, as was his usual haunt, but staring right at him with an open face and wide eyes.

"Save me," he said.

The sound of his voice was so real. It *was* real. He actually heard the sound of it...and it frightened him more than looking down.

"Are you OK, Trask?" James shouted from below.

"I'm fine," he shouted down.

"Find the survivors," James yelled.

"OK," Trask said shakily. "OK."

Two men were found alive: the cook, who had been calling incessantly for rescue, and the first mate, though his body was so frozen Trask could barely unwind it from the main mast. Trask found three other bodies. The rest had been washed overboard, or had died in a futile attempt to swim to shore.

The cook stepped into the foothold. He made the sign of the cross on his chest as he was lowered.

"*Grazie Angelo!*" he said, over and over again on his way down.

Trask tied the first mate around the chest and feet. The crew lowered him like cargo into the boat. Expectations were low all around on his chance for survival.

"The rest are dead, sir," Trask shouted to James below.

"Then lower yourself," James replied. "We'll come back for them in the morning."

James had done a masterful job keeping *Audacious* in position, but when Trask lowered himself into the vessel, the boat seemed too full by half. Mannering bailed frantically to buoy the vessel.

"Starboard! Pull! Now, together men. Pull!"

But with more bodies in the boat, it became harder to coordinate their efforts at navigation. James tried to stay within the shadow of the wreck, but as *Audacious* moved away, the wave action got heavier. Not more than 200 yards from shore, the vessel blasted into a gray and foam-speckled behemoth that threw the boat like a cork. It remained afloat, but athwart the waves now, the men were defenseless from a broadside.

"Starboard, pull! Port, reverse!" James tried to right the vessel quickly, but the men were shook, and out of sync. The inevitable rose up quickly off the sandy bottom like a black wall, drooling foam from its caps, and loaded with ice chunks of up to 2,000 pounds.

One of the men screamed as they were all jettisoned from their perches into the soapy brew. The wave rammed the boat in after them.

They were lost to each other instantly.

The rescuers suddenly found they were in the unlucky position of requiring rescue themselves...

Chapter Fifty

Save!

Occasionally, the veil of sleet would part, and Century would glimpse the scene out past the breakers. *Audacious*, being white, would appear for a moment. He could see it was having difficulty staying athwart ship.

Sounds broke through the torrent, clues. Though the specific words were indecipherable, the tenor of James' commands indicated that all was not going well.

Reef, Century's only companion on the beach, was turning himself inside-out with worry. He paced in circles, sat for an anxious moment or two, then continued his pacing, all the time looking out toward the boats. Occasionally, an anxious *yowl* would leap from the depths of his throat, almost against his will to control it.

Century was pacing, too, to keep warm. Because of their long hunt down the beach, James had forgone the lighting of a fire. In this weather, it would be a fair trick, in any case. But it was the one thing Abraham Century yearned for at this moment, to hear the *hiss* and *crackle* of a fire well-fed...

"Bng a yrd est tor d'ort."

It was the voice of James...but what was he saying? Century looked out, without motion, fairly cocking his ears as Reef did. The two of them, like gargoyles in the rain, listening.

After a time, Century starting bobbing up and down again on his toes, and wrapping his arms around his chest.

"Whew, it's cold..." he said to Reef who looked up at him for a moment, whined anxiously, and looked out again into the darkness over the waves...

Reef pranced forward as the waves receded. He barked and howled wildly, coming out of his skin in frustration, because he couldn't dare the waves.

"Stay boy!" said Abraham Century. He hadn't heard much from the crew in a while.

Had the boat capsized? He imagined the men clinging to the craft, and floating somewhere free in this slop.

He squinted hard into the slurry, and saw what he thought were two men swimming for shore. Suddenly, he saw *Audacious*, upside-down!

He waded in until, at a standing tide, the water was at his neck. He grabbed one of the men, Slocum, and headed back to the beach. A hollow thud of water smacked the back of his head. He held onto Slocum, and pulled him up to safety where Reef started licking his face.

He turned to re-enter the maelstrom.

Some of the crew had righted themselves, and were coming up the beach, but some were still clearly missing. Century grabbed another body, this one tangled in cordage. It was Mannering, blue with cold, and shivering uncontrollably.

"LET GO OF THE LINES!!!!" Century screamed, but Mannering didn't seem to hear him.

His eyes only rolled back in his head. Another wave rolled over them, and for several moments Century couldn't feel the bottom with his feet. He and Mannering were floating together, outward away from the beach, carried by the sinewy pull of the outgoing tide. A surge of panic bolted through Century, and he started to flail his arms in a vain attempt to swim. His head dipped under the surface again, and he inhaled a mouthful of seawater. He screamed underwater, and the odd sound of it surprised him, and seemed to snap him to.

When the water receded a bit, Century got his footing. He pulled his knife out of its sheath, and began cutting the cords that held him to this dying man. It was like wrestling with a giant octopus, but, after several thrashing motions, he cut himself free. His efforts freed Mannering as well, so he grabbed the limp body by the arm, and pulled it behind him on his way in.

"Gilbert is still out there," said John Barker, grabbing Mannering from Century as he emerged from the surf.

Century turned for a third time, and looked out into the surf. He couldn't see Gilbert. The man was probably already dead, and Century was panting like a steam engine. His body felt like petrified wood. A quick look at the spent and limp bodies on the beach was enough to know that no one else was capable at that moment to attempt the rescue.

Century grabbed a loose rope, and tied it around his waist. Then he waded into the surf up to his chest and disappeared...

Barker looked out into the storm, but was met with a blizzard of white noise, a torrent of static that had rushed in to fill, obscure, and now threaten, the very memory of the man, so lately a stout colleague, now...The unbroken roar of the storm remained, blotting out the space Century filled, even his shadow, swallowed.

Out there?

Suddenly, Century grew in stature, larger even than in life.

An ice block of unholy prospect lolled about in the churning shallows like St. Peter at the gates of heaven. None might enter other than those called.

"Century!!!" Barker called. "Century!!!"

Reef barked and growled viciously, and finally, when he could stand it no longer, pranced pathetically into the surf. The raw energy of a gathering monster immediately punished the dog, lifting him up and into its sinewy curl, and spewing him mercilessly backward. It followed with a pummeling Reef could not understand, spilling its momentum gathered from the fetch of the wind over the Atlantic. The dog struggled to maintain his head above water, then sank, and was completely submerged by the white froth of the sea.

The wave withdrew, leaving Reef struggling to regain his

footing in the rapidly receding water. He leapt forward toward the beach, and shook himself furiously. Then, he padded over toward the other men, having completely forgotten why he had leapt into the water in the first place.

Chapter Fifty-One

I Want To Go Home

Dere's no rain to wet you,
O, yes I want to go home.

Irregular run the patterns on the polished gray-steel waters, bubbling up endlessly from some hidden font.

Dere's no sun to burn you,
O, yes I want to go home;

And there are the little Piping Plovers, busy about their day, hustling in after the waves recede, picking up little scraps of food, carried in by the surf. Then, like miserly little people, scampering back up the beach when the next wave returns.

O, push along, believers,
O, yes I want to go home;

And the wave retires softly into the sand, leaving behind a broad impression - air bubbles perculating up through. A sign of life? Or merely air trapped below?

Dere's no hard trials,
O, yes I want to go home;

And the Least Terns circle and wheel overhead. One stops, poised and hovering in the air, spying a darting school of killies in the surf. It dives straight down, splashing head-first into the water. After a brief tussle, the predator emerges into the air, with a prize in its beak, a fresh kill, still wriggling with life. It squawks in defiance at the other birds. "*I am the bird who has caught the fish,*" it seems to say. "*I am the one. Look at me. I am the bird who has caught the fish.*"

> *Der's no whips a-crackin',*
> *O, yes I want to go home;*
>
> *My brudder on de wayside,*
> *O, yes I want to go home;*
>
> *O, push along, my brudder,*
> *O, yes I want to go home;*
>
> *Where der's no stormy weather,*
> *O, yes I want to go home;*
>
> *Dere's no tribulation,*
> *O, yes I want to go home.*

Epilogue

The Funeral of Abraham Century

When Cassandra and Dahlia arrived, Trask was standing atop a beach dune, leaning on his crutch, looking out over the wide expanse of the calm but cold bay. Reef, like a mountain, sat upright next to him.

From behind, Cassandra studied Trask for a moment. His bleached white hair close-cropped to his head set off his tan and heavily creased neck. His relaxed and gallant posture electrified the landscape.

They were both loath to break his reverie, but Reef soon turned his head, and trotted toward the ladies, happy tail flailing.

"Hey, Reef," Cassandra called out happily, "How's my puppy?"

Trask turned to her.

"I'm glad you could make it."

"You know us, we can't stay away," Cassandra replied coyly.

The threesome began walking toward the graveyard where the service was to be held just a few hundred yards away at the end of this path back through the woods.

Cassandra's white skin and red hair were set off neatly by a black, wide-brimmed hat, tied underneath with some sheer black fabric. He squeezed her hands as he kissed her offered cheek.

Dahlia, on the other hand, looked utterly inconsolable. Even beneath the crimped black veil that covered her face, Trask could see that her skin was several shades paler than normal. Her eyes looked like they had been the aqueducts of tears for weeks.

Trask put his hand on her shoulder.

"Have you heard," Trask said entering daintily into the conversation that attends these events. "They're burying him on land."

"Well, he never was much of a swimmer," Dahlia replied. Then, realizing the implications of such an awkward statement, she burst into tears.

"It's OK," Cassandra said, tapping her on the arm.

"No. It's no use," she said between sobs. "It's no use. I can't do it. I can't go through with this. Take me back. Please, M's Wolff. Take me back."

Cassandra and Trask exchanged a furtive glance. The strength of her reaction surprised them. She had known Abraham Century. She had clearly cared for him. But *this*...

This was a grief suffered for all young men who die before their time, bravely and in the service of others. This was a grief for everyone who has been loved and cared for, who has shared this life, this space in our hearts, in our lives, who is then suddenly gone, leaving only echoes...

Dahlia buried her face into Cassandra's shoulder. The tears came with such a force, there seemed to be no limit to the volume. The three stopped on their way, knowing the service was about to begin. Yet, for Dahlia, to arrive in this state was unseemly. Her tears seemed to be coming from some inexhaustible reservoir deep in her interior, and there was no telling when, or if, they would end.

"Dahlia," Cassandra said firmly. "Look at my face."

Dahlia did not.

Cassandra put her hand under Dahlia's chin, and raised it up to hers. Dahlia's eyes still resisted, looking down and away.

"Look at my face, Dahlia."

Through a force of effort her eyes relented, and slowly came around to look into Cassandra's. Cassandra's face blanched at this direct encounter with such grief. Dahlia eyes were completely lost, swimming somewhere far out in a sea of tears.

"Dahlia..."

"It's no use...It's no use ...I loved him, M's Wolff. I loved him..."

With that her head descended again into Cassandra's shoulder, and she wailed like a six-year-old girl. Cassandra enfolded her arms completely around her, and gently patted her on the back. She gestured with her head for Trask to go on ahead.

Trask complied, leaving the two sobbing together on this forlorn walkway through the dune trees. It wasn't far for Trask to walk through the last craggy archway made by the windswept pines, and out into the open area behind the churchyard.

Already the ceremony had begun, and the mourners were assembled around the wooden cask that held the body of Abraham Century. Joshua James stood by, his hands hanging awkwardly at his sides, looking out of context, dressed in his only suit, an ill-fitting number that he dusted off for these occasions.

Some black people from the town were grouped together, huddled against the cold. They were gracious, but, like James, seemed so out of place exposed like this, in the cold churchyard down by the bay beach.

The preacher spoke: "We return Abraham Century now into the arms of the Lord from which he came. He stayed with us for all too short a time, but we will remember him well as a man of stout heart and strong back. May the Lord have mercy on his soul, and may all the angels of heaven welcome him with open arms."

With that short statement, the men lifted the heavy casket, and, using three heavy ship hawsers, lowered the body of Abraham Century into the grave. Two men with shovels tenderly filled the hole, and, as each gentle shovelful was hove atop the box, the ladies in the assemblage hurt a little more.

They clutched handkerchiefs against their cheeks, the soft cloth like remnants of human love in a cold world of sand and iron.

When the last shovelful was ladled upon him, two men brought out a headstone upon which was carved an epitaph. Joshua James removed his lifesavers' cap, stepped forward, and read the inscription:

> *In this grave from the wide ocean doth sleep*
> *The bodies of those that had crossed the deep*
> *And instead of being landed safe on the shore*
> *In a cold frosty night they all were no more.*
>
> *Abraham Century*
> *1820 - 1858*

Trask noticed Cassandra and Dahlia had entered the periphery of the group, afraid to come too close to the source of their grief. Reef stood like a guardian at their side. Overhead a seagull yawped, and circled the assemblage in sympathy.

James went on with some personal remarks: "Abraham Century died with a lifesavers' line in this hands. We've buried him with that line, still in his right hand..."

James paused, a surge of emotion threatening to overtake his stoic demeanor. He teetered for a moment, like a ship suspended at the apex of a wave's crest, on the verge of tipping into a swale of sorrow. The small crowd was suspended there with him, not breathing, it seemed, until he could continue. James stretched his neck out of his starched collar, cleared his throat, and forged ahead.

"Abraham Century...once said to me...'When I see a man clinging to a wreck...I see nothing else in the world... and I never think of family and friends...until I have saved him...' "

Gasps of emotion rippled through the crowd. Dahlia plowed her head back into Cassandra's shoulder, and sobbed without shame.

"That is the essence of the man we bury today...Let us never forget him or what he stood for."

"Amen," the black ladies all said. "Hallelujah."

They all sang together a mournful dirge.

> *De little baby gone home,*
> *De little baby gone home,*
> *De little baby gone along,*
> *For to climb up Jacob's ladder.*
> *And I wish I'd been dar,*
> *I wish I'd been dar,*
> *I wish I'd been dar, my Lord,*
> *For to climb up Jacob's ladder.*

James then signaled to Trask who turned to the Lyle gun, aimed into the bay, and lit the fuse. The flame skipped directly into the bronze canon, which kicked back with a mighty blast. The mourners were silent as they listened to the sound reverberate over the bay, echoing into ever broadening circles, then fading away into faint ringlets of memory...

In life, what James had given to Abraham Century was simple enough. He recognized him as an American - fully free, fully responsible, fully human. He expected him to give his all, which he expected from everyone.

Century had responded in full measure; he *did* give his all, indeed, his very life.

In death, James had given Century another precious gift - a legacy, a way for him to live on.

And now, as long as there are human hearts engaged in the joys and sorrows of life, the strength and courage of Abraham Century will live forever.

Amen.

About the Author

John J. Stevens loves telling stories about the waterfront.

He is the Writer – Director of three public television documenaries:

Freedom's Glory: The Restoration of the Little Jennie, the story of one man's obsessive quest to restore the Chesapeake Bay oyster dredger, *Little Jennie;*

How Sound is Long Island Sound? about the ecological condition of Long Island Sound;

Alive in An Urban Harbor, about the revival of species in New York Harbor.

A Long Island native, Stevens currently lives a five-minute drive from where he was born. He is the Founder and President of Bullfrog Communications, Inc. a digital communications company.

Fire Island is his first novel.

About the Illustrations

The illustrations in the book are almost entirely stock photos of images published in periodicals of the time, particularly *Harper's Weekly*. The style of these images is known as *line engraving*, or simply *engraving*.

The engravings were made by an artist who would by hand meticulously carve the lines which comprise the image into a block of wood. After ink is applied to the carved block, it is used to impress an image to paper.

It's a wonderful graphic style that is sadly fading away.

Bibliography

Adams III, Charles J., and David J. Seibold. *Shipwrecks Off Ocean City* Reading: Exeter House Books, 1986. Print.

Berg, Daniel. *Wreck Valley: A Record Of Shipwrecks Off Long Island's South Shore*. Lynbrook, New York: Aqua Explorers, Inc., 1986. Print.

Buchholz, Margaret Thomas. *New Jersey Shipwrecks: 350 years in the Graveyard of the Atlantic*. Harvey Cedars, New Jersey: Down The Shore Publishing, 2004. Print.

Burrows, Edwin G., and Mike Wallace. *Gotham: A History of New York City to 1898*. New York: Oxford University Press, USA, 1998. Print.

Cartography Associates. "Historical Map Collection." David Rumsey Map Collection. N.p., n.d. Web. 20 July 2010. <www.davidrumsey.com >.

Field, Van R. *Wrecks and Rescues On Long Island*. Stated 1st Edition. Center Moriches, New York: Searles Graphics, 1997. Print.

Johnson, Madeline C. *Fire Island: 1650's- 1980's*. Mountainside, New Jersey: Shoreland Press, 1983. Print.

Matthiessen, Peter. *Men's Lives: The Surfmen and Baymen of the South Fork*. New York: Random House, 1986. Print.

McKay, Richard C. *South Street: A Maritime History Of New York*. 2nd Edition. New York, New York: 7 C's Press, 1969. Print.

Merryman, John Henry. *United States Life-Saving Service: 1880*. 1st Paper, 1st Printing ed. Grand Junction, Colorado: Outbooks, 1989. Print.

Noble, Dennis L. *That Others Might Live: The U.S. Life-Saving Service, 1878-1915*. Annapolis, Md: Naval Institute Press, 1994. Print.

Squires, Donald F. *Sea Grant Maritime Heritage Series: The Bight of the Big Apple*. Albany, New York: New York Sea Grant Institute, 1981. Print.

JUL  2013

CPSIA information can be obtained at www.ICGtesting.com
Printed in the USA
LVOW072207210613

339641LV00001B/132/P